The
Thin Tear
in the
Fabric of
Space

The

Iowa

Short

Fiction

Award

In memory of my sister, Jolee

Peace, tender sapling, thou art made of tears,

And tears will quickly melt thy life away.

—WILLIAM SHAKESPEARE, Titus Andronicus

Contents

ACKNOWLEDGMENTS

I am grateful to the publications listed below for their permission to reprint the following stories, earlier versions of which first appeared in their pages: "Saint Francis in Flint," the *Paris Review* (Spring/Summer 2001); "Central Square," the *New England Review* (Summer 2002); "The River," *Glimmer Train* (Winter 2002); "Fellowship of the Bereaved," *Fugue* (Winter 2003); "Girls I Know," *Epoch* (Fall 2004); "The Surprising Weight of the Body's Organs," *Epoch* (Summer 2005); and "The Thin Tear in the Fabric of Space," the *Black Warrior Review* (Fall 2005).

I also wish to thank the many writers, editors, and friends who gave me such valuable feedback while I wrote these stories: Susan Burmeister-Brown, Stephen Clark, Robert Cohen, Stephen Donadio, Ben George, David Hamilton, Brigid Hughes, Michael Koch, Kevin Kopelson, Tom Lutz, Thomas Mallon, Joyce Carol Oates, George Plimpton, Jodee Stanley Rubins, Raymond Smith, and Linda B. Swanson-Davies. At the University of Iowa Press, I would like to thank Holly Carver, Karen Copp, Sara Sauers, and Charlotte Wright. My appreciation goes out especially to Miriam Altshuler, my agent and friend, to my wife Theresa, for her insights and patience, and to my parents and my son, William.

While researching "Labor Day Hurricane, 1935," I found the following books and articles to be particularly helpful: Willie Drye's *Storm of the Century* (National Geographic Society, 2002), Garry Boulard's "State of Emergency: Key West in the Great Depression" (*Florida Historical Quarterly*, vol. 67, no. 2, 1988), Les Standiford's *Last Train to Paradise* (Three Rivers Press, 2002), and the *Guide to Key West* compiled by workers of the Writers' Program of the Work Projects Administration in the State of Florida (Hastings House, New York, 1941).

The
Thin Tear
in the
Fabric of
Space

The
Thin Tear
in the
Fabric of
Space

Elena Gavrushnekov made her way slowly into the Physics Department of Excellence University, through the heavy iron doors inlaid with thick glass, right up to the desk of Patti Tipendorf, the freshly minted, work-study receptionist who would be answering the phones for the spring semester. Elena walked timidly, not trusting her legs, which buckled and wobbled beneath her. In her left hand she clutched a piece of yellowed stationery on which she had written an acrostic in the form of a kind of bogus, verbal equation: her version of a *carpe diem* poem.

"Good morning . . . that is, hello there . . . darling." Elena smiled, reminding herself not to let her lips part, lest Patti glimpse her crooked, discolored teeth.

"Hi, Professor Gavrushnekov." Patti tripped awkwardly over the middle syllables of her last name. "How is your project going?"

"Well, I am p-pleased to announce that I have brought it . . . well, yes, I may say . . . brought it to completion. Would today be a good day f-for . . . for our coffee? P-Perhaps in a half-hour or so? I can save a . . . save a—of course—a table, f-for us." Elena's voice, difficult for her to control in the first place, now teetered precipitously between a whisper and a wail.

"I think so. Let me . . ." Patti pulled a pink plastic DayTimer out of her purse, recently purchased for the new semester, and opened to the date, marked by a heart-shaped paper clip. As Elena knew, Patti had a half-hour coffee break in the morning, and an hour off for lunch. "Yes, that would be fine."

"Wonderful. I will, at long last . . . that is, yes . . . at long last explain my work to you."

"And I'll print out my résumé."

"Oh by all means. And to whet your . . . as it were, to . . . so-licit . . . oh goodness, wrong word . . . to *invigorate* your appe-tite f-for our discussion, yes, that's right, I have written a small *note*—" she attempted a wink but the left side of her face resisted the gesture—"for your perusal."

Having clenched her fingers, Elena did not have the muscle control required to release the piece of paper. She raised her arm, now in full flutter, onto the desk. Patti Tipendorf gently pulled the folded paper out of her hand. A student slumped in the far corner of the office, waiting for his registration card to be signed, watched the exchange.

"Thank you, Miss Tipendorf."

Patti smiled. For a moment Elena stared dumbly at the girl's face, its foldless skin, the cheeks rounded and full, frosted with just a touch of pink. Then, in spite of her efforts otherwise, she could not stop her eyes from peering down at Patti's tremen-dous breasts, which pressed up against her red cashmere sweater. These were breasts that had yet to feel the downward tug of grav-ity: beautiful, pert breasts. Looking at them, Elena was unable to suppress yet another thin smile. She turned abruptly from the desk, embarrassed, mumbled thanks again, and then began what would be for her the long walk to the coffee shop on Excellence

Drive, just across the central quad from the Physics Department. It would take her nearly ten minutes to cover the distance, about three hundred yards.

After she was gone, Patti unfolded the piece of stationery and read the following:

L aw of Missing Energy

O mega, the figure by which we name all of matter in the cosmos, when combined with the

V elocity of our expanding, isotropic universe, tells us that

E nergy in our galaxies is missing, along with the

M ass of many stars, and the

E mission lines we would expect to emanate from some of our larger nebulae.

P hysicists who claim dark matter as an explanation

A dd, when pressed, the curvature of space as another cause.

T hese same men know that 90% of our universe remains unaccounted for, and

T hat the Hawking radiation emitted by black holes cannot make up the difference.

I s there perhaps a thin tear in the fabric of space?

Missing the acrostic entirely, Patti shook her head with bewilderment and put the paper in her purse.

"What's it say?" The student seated in the corner lifted his baseball cap and put it back on his head. He had been trying to make eye contact with Patti for several minutes before Elena Gavrushnekov had entered, and her exit had given him an excuse to speak.

"It's like a poem, kind of . . ." In the last week alone, Patti had received half a dozen of Elena's notes, but had yet to read any of them as amorous declarations.

"She is *so* into you."

Patti didn't say anything.

"What's with the shakes? Is she a drunk or something?"

"I don't know. I think she's unwell."

"Dude, she's *all* into you."

Patti shook her head, blushing, her dyed blond hair pushing up against her headband. "She said she'd write me a letter of recommendation for the School of Education if I had coffee with her. She said she'd explain her theory of the cosmos and write a letter for me. I told her that I don't know anything about science but she said it wouldn't matter, that I'd understand it anyway. She's a professor, she was a professor, in the English Department, but she knows about physics too. She thinks I'd make a good high school teacher."

The boy shrugged. "She was all, like, *into you*," he mumbled.

Patti returned to her clerical work: posting the office hours of all the physics professors on the department Web site. She was still unaware that she had in fact been the inspiration for the completion of Elena Gavrushnekov's cosmology, her study of the structure and composition of the universe. Neither did Patti know, although this she suspected, that Elena Gavrushnekov's brain was badly damaged, and that her days remaining as an animate being on this planet, in this solar system, in this galaxy, were very few.

Patti Tipendorf was right about Elena Gavrushnekov's employment status. The professor—an expert on the work of mid Romantic, feminist poets but only barely known in the field, as the two articles she had published were not widely cited—was on permanent medical leave from Excellence University. Her health problems went back to the spring of 2000, when she began to suffer excruciating headaches directly behind her right eye. Elena first dismissed these headaches as grief induced, caused by the death of Dmitri, her former husband. And so she took greater and greater doses, first of Tylenol, then Advil, then Excedrin, and finally varying mixtures of all three, until—now barely able to get out of bed in the morning—Casha, her lover and companion, pointed out that grief was an unlikely cause for her suffering, since Dmitri had tormented both of them with harassing phone calls and icy stares in the supermarket for years. "The man was a Neanderthal," she reminded Elena. "What was there possibly to mourn?"

Casha recommended a trip to the doctor and Elena refused, until the severity of her headaches made it impossible for her even to eat, much less take care of her vegetable garden. When she finally paid a visit to the Excellence University Health Clinic, the neurologist on call asked her a series of questions and then ordered a CAT scan that revealed a tumor about the size of a walnut pressing sharply against her olfactory nerve. Subsequent tests identified the tumor as benign, and a tricky extraction surgery, in which damage to the brain was a distinct possibility, was scheduled.

In fact, the seven-hour surgery was a great success: the tumor was removed without damaging any of the nerves that controlled Elena's facial features, so she did not develop the droopy mouth or eyelid condition commonly suffered by brain-surgery survivors. The following week, Casha booked roundtrip airplane tickets for them from Excellence to Seattle, and a berth on a cruise ship that would take them from the Pacific Northwest up along the Alaska coastline and then back to Washington State.

They never took the trip. About a month after the surgery, Elena began to act oddly. First she spoke to Casha in Russian, mistaking her for her Aunt Lavanya. Then she put on her gardening clothes and said she had to weed, even though their small backyard was covered with snow. Finally she burst into song, Brünnhilde's seventeen-minute aria from the end of Wagner's *Götterdämmerung*, and Casha knew something was wrong: no Russian in her right mind would sing Wagner. So she rushed her partner to the emergency room, where it was determined that Elena had fluid buildup in the cavity created by the removal of her tumor. In an emergency surgery the next day, a neurosurgeon inserted a shunt to drain this fluid from her brain, through her neck, into her stomach. Elena felt better briefly, and then started acting oddly again, asking Casha to help her dress for the funeral of her Uncle Leopold, who had died in 1974, and then suddenly announcing plans to take the train from Moscow to Beijing, even if that meant rejoining the Communist Party.

It took an additional six surgeries before a shunt with the appropriate drainage valve was found: one that permitted neither an infinitesimal buildup of fluid to occur, nor overhasty drainage, as both states resulted in delusions, loss of memory, and—over time—permanent dementia. After demonstrating no odd behavior for three days, Elena was released from the clinic. For many months she felt fine: weaker than before, certainly, but mentally sound. Then she began to feel an odd tingle in her right hand, and then her left, followed by periods of numbness and then twitching. Incrementally, over the course of the next few months, use of her hands, then her forearms, and finally her legs became increasingly difficult. Elena knew something was wrong but did not consider seeing a doctor, even though she was spending most of her days in the waiting room of the health clinic. Casha had been diagnosed with late-term breast cancer. In her early fifties, she had never had a mammogram. She died in intense pain, having refused both sedatives and painkillers. "I want to feel this," she tried to explain between anguished cries. "I want to feel how life ends." She died clutching Elena's fingers in one hand, and the rosary given to her by her mother when she had been a girl growing up in Warsaw in the other.

Crouched over her lover's bed, her hand turned purple by Casha's grip, Elena felt nothing, at least in her arm. A week later she burned herself badly when she dropped her teakettle on the stovetop. Back in the clinic, a series of tests confirmed that she suffered from a rare condition, perhaps a result of her numerous brain surgeries but just as likely not, that caused deterioration of the nerves along her spinal cord. There was no cure for arachnoidal cell fibrosis, and while one of the neurosurgeons at the clinic recommended a procedure in which he and another doctor would have actually scraped the stricken cells from her spinal column, two other doctors on the same staff thought the procedure was too dangerous. "You can risk immediate paralysis," one of them explained, "or you can face the possibility of one day losing the use of your arms and legs." "One day soon?" Elena had asked. "Three to five years," the doctor replied. "Well, I could be struck by a bus in three to five years," she had responded. "I could be run over by a student on his mountain bike, with those ridiculously large wheels. I shall, I believe, take my chances."

The neurologist nodded, then continued. "There's more news. Fluid trauma to your frontal and temporal lobes has resulted in permanent damage to your brain tissue."

"Brain *damage*?" she had whispered in response.

"Irreversible and degenerative," the doctor added, the folder holding her x-rays, CAT scans, and other charts spilling out before him. "I'm afraid it will only get worse."

"I know the meaning of *degenerative*," she had snapped.

This had all happened three years before. Since that time, Elena had ceased not only her work as a literary critic but also her bedtime reading of Pushkin. She had instead devoted her energies to the study of the universe and the development of her own private theory about immortality, dark matter, and the space-time continuum. This was the project to which she referred as being completed, a project inspired in part by her encroaching death but also by her ex-husband Dmitri, a physicist of some renown whose notebooks she had managed to procure from his second wife after his unexpected death on a pheasant hunt in the fields just north of campus (he had not been shot but instead had managed to fall into a ditch, strike his head hard against a drainage pipe, and drown in seven inches of mud). Having shown dazzling mathematical skills as a younger man, Dmitri had been hired by Excellence—with Elena in tow—on the basis of his unorthodox view that the rate of the universe's expansion was actually increasing: an implausible contention, although one that would finally be proven by the Hubble Space Telescope eight years after his death. Elena hoped to find, in his notebooks, clues to Dmitri's own thinking about the cosmos. What was revealed instead was that her ex-husband had spent the last three years of his life trying to design a machine that could film a person's dreams.

We really weren't that different, she thought as she opened the door to Fresh Roast, the coffee shop across the street from campus. Yes, Dmitri was a Neanderthal, Casha was right, but he wanted to find answers to the most important questions one can ask: questions far more provocative than "Is there a God?" Dmitri wanted to know what constituted the difference between matter and fantasy, between the end of time and the eternality of energy. He was, all in all, a good Russian. And Casha was, in spite of her homosexuality, a good Pole, a good Catholic.

Elena ordered her coffee black and headed for the table in the corner of the shop, nestled between the windows facing the sidewalk and the interior wall. Jason, the barista working that afternoon was, like so many young people in retail and restaurant jobs in town, a former English major. We humanists teach them everything we know, Elena had thought more than once, and then they find themselves unsuitable for any meaningful employment in society. He brought her coffee over to her after it had been individually drip-brewed into a ceramic mug, and left her there to wait for Patti Tipendorf.

To pass the time, Elena pulled from her purse the folded pages of notes on which her cosmology was written and set them down on the table. She was desperate to communicate to Patti what she had been thinking about these last three years, but she knew it would be difficult. Not only was Elena's speech severely hampered by her condition, which forced awkward pauses and persistent stuttering over initial hard consonants, but Patti was, as far as she could tell, a very stupid young girl. She was young and beautiful and dazzlingly, splendidly stupid in a way that only American youths were stupid: stupid with a smile on her face, stupid in her determination to learn, in her matching lipstick and sweater outfits. But it worked both ways. Patti's stupidity might make it impossible for her to grasp Elena's cosmological discovery, but at the same time, Patti was just stupid enough to listen to her, a doddering old lady, enfeebled by a mysterious disease. One would have to be quite stupid to take her seriously, this Elena knew. This she knew not in spite of, but because her brain was quite seriously damaged by now. She had first been surprised, then horrified, to learn that brain damage did not necessarily wipe out your capacity to analyze yourself. You could, if you were unlucky enough, have the capacity to chart your own cerebral decay. It was ironic, she thought, no it was *paradoxical*, that at this juncture, in her final effort to explain to her own satisfaction why she no longer dreamed of her beloved Casha, at this moment when she felt breathlessly close to disproving the cosmological validity of all Cartesian thinking, it was at this moment paradoxically that the corroding tissue of Elena's brain was making any lucid assertion of the indistinguishability of body and spirit that much harder to put forward. On the cusp of dealing gravity a deathblow by revealing the thin tear in the fabric of space into which spirits like Casha, spirits defiant of the God of Man, had fled, Elena was being crushed, savagely and brutally, by the sun's hideous pull on earth, which was literally tearing the nerves on her spinal column into bits. Or at least that's how she understood—without sedatives or painkillers—what it feels like when your life is ending.

Patti arrived a half-hour later. In her hand she carried a manila folder and in the folder a fresh, laser-printed copy of her résumé. On the front of the folder she had clipped a blank piece of paper.

Patti wasn't sure if Professor Gavrushnekov might expect her to take notes on her theory of the universe and didn't want to arrive unprepared. She had never had coffee with a professor before. In fact, she could count on one hand the number of times that she had spotted one of her teachers off campus. In the small midwestern town in which she had grown up, there hadn't been people like Elena Gavrushnekov: people with foreign accents and advanced degrees who knew very important things that had to be explained in lecture halls—ideas that somehow managed to make perfect sense when they were heard but hardly any sense once they were copied down and reread during exam week. Patti was not a good student; her grades were mostly Cs, except in the required science and math courses, where they were Ds, but Professor Gavrushnekov had clearly seen potential, telling her, just minutes into their first conversation, that she'd make an excellent elementary school teacher and that she'd write a recommendation that said just that, if Patti wanted her to.

"P-Please, p-please." Elena gestured toward the empty chair on the other side of the table. "Such an . . . an absolute p-pleasure. Such a p-pleasure."

Patti set her mug of coffee down on the table, next to her folder, and took a seat.

"And are you f-finding . . . have you f-found the Ph-Physics Department . . . or rather have you *become* . . . that is . . . accustomed to your p-place of . . . employment?"

Patti glanced around for a moment, as if hoping that someone sitting nearby would lean over and restate the question for her. "Yes, it's a good job. Not too busy."

"Well, the department is not . . . that is . . . it is not really . . . not very good." Elena had leaned her head back on her neck so that it would twitch less, but this meant that she was no longer looking at Patti as much as the ceiling above her. "I take it you know . . . I mean to say . . . P-Professor Wilkins?"

"Yeah, he hired me. He's the chair." The familiar-sounding name was enough for Patti to lapse momentarily into her natural way of speaking, but she caught herself quickly.

"The man is . . . well he is . . . that is, P-Professor Wilkins is a degenerate p-pervert. He has . . . I dare say . . . tried to . . . mount . . . or, that is . . . he has attempted to . . . *p-penetrate* his assistants in the past. I would recommend avoiding . . . yes . . . staying away from . . . that is . . . avoiding at all costs, his office. I would see him only in . . . in p-public p-places." Elena took a sip of her coffee, now room temperature, by holding the mug with both hands.

Patti's eyebrows, plucked into thin lines, wrinkled in confusion. She had been expecting to hear about Professor Gavrushnekov's theory of the universe and then, hopefully, discuss her application to the School of Education. She didn't realize that Elena had already begun describing her cosmology. She looked intently at the professor's narrow head, the skin white and wrinkled, the hair above her ears and forehead wispy and gray. Patti thought Professor Gavrushnekov resembled a certain kind of bird, the name of which she couldn't recall. It was a bird they had studied in her evolutionary biology class.

"I make a p-point," Elena continued, "each semester . . . I make sure to drop by so as to . . . that is, to warn . . . one might say, to *caution* the new receptionist. Just issue a gentle notice . . . one might say . . . f-from one woman to another. Men like P-Professor Wilkins, these men are . . . shall I say . . . *animated* by a . . . by an appetite f-for . . . for young women. These men are very much . . . very much . . . that is, even their regard for the cosmos is . . . qualified . . . no, *compromised* by . . . no, *compensatory* for . . . that is, dictated by their p-pathetic sex drives and their . . . really unimaginable ignorance of the f-feminine . . . to quote a contemporary . . . the f-feminine mystique. Would a f-female ph-physicist . . . would she have called it the *Big Bang Theory*? I think not."

Elena tried to laugh but when she opened her mouth no sound came out. She looked down at her notes, the scribblings a mix of English and Russian that—owing to her lack of muscle control—were layered on top of one another and impossible to read. She tried as best she could to gather her thoughts while Patti took a red fountain pen out of her purse.

"In the science that I have been writing in my head," Elena glanced down again, "mostly in my head, there is . . . there is no meaningful distinction between ph-physical and psychic ph-phenomena. That is . . . if I may use an . . . an example . . . a chair might weigh the same as the memory of eating . . . of eating flavored ice as a little girl in Bitsevsky P-Park in Moscow. This science of which . . . of which I speak . . . it cannot be written down . . . or even spoken . . . in our current world. We would f-first need . . . shall I say . . . we would need a large redistribution of . . . of income. We would certainly . . . we would have to have . . . there would need to be a f-female p-president of this country. We would need to . . . there could be no more things like . . . f-football for instance. Or ice hockey. In the language that would truly . . . truly express this science, there would be no metaphor or . . . or wordplay. The tear that I suspect exists . . . is p-present in . . . a p-part of . . . the f-fabric of space could only signify a rip. It could not impart an affect . . . an *evocation* as it were, of grief. Am I making myself at all understood?"

Patti stared at Professor Gavrushnekov's open mouth: the teeth crooked and yellow, with intricate, metal bridgework visible in the corners of her jaw. She had not followed a word of what the woman had said but she had still managed to write down a phrase here and there.

"I should have begun," Elena shut her eyes, then opened them again, "I should have made it clear . . . at the outset . . . that . . . well, let me begin again. Have you heard of . . . of Alexander F-Friedmann? No. Well then, he was the f-first . . . the first to p-prove mathematically that the universe was expanding. Dmitri . . . my . . . shall I say, violent and . . . perhaps one might say . . . *sociopathic* husband, studied with him at P-Petrograd, and was able to calculate mathematically . . . that is, he could show that the universe was expanding and also curved. Have you heard of Einstein? Yes? Good. Well . . . Einstein p-proved that gravity . . . that is, that gravity is not . . . not so much a f-force but rather an effect of . . . a p-product of . . . no a *f-feature* of multiple dimensions. Therefore, it is p-possible to construct . . . through general relativity . . . it is p-possible to imagine a tear in the f-fabric of space. An escape from time . . . from the expanse of the universe. And an escape from dimensions."

Patti nodded her head as she wrote. Professor Gavrushnekov continued.

"I buried my Casha, my love . . ." Elena's voice caught and for a moment she thought she might lose her balance and fall to the floor, but she regained her composure. "For a year I dreamed of . . . of Casha. I grieved her p-passing as one might . . . as one in my p-place should have. I cried in my sleep. I wore her . . . her f-frayed . . . her blue nightgown. I drank my . . . my breakfast tea with her mug from the . . . from the Chicago Art Institute. I f-fed her . . . her hostile cat. Then I f-felt my grief slip away somewhere and I . . . I began to study and . . . construct . . . no, *theorize* as it were, my cosmology."

Elena reached a limp, shaking hand across the table and set it down on top of Patti's pen. "Heaven is not clouds and gates," she said. "It is light. It is matter . . . it is matter transformed into light. It is a p-place . . . a p-place outside of space and time in which there is no difference between light and matter. It is through the tear . . . the tear of which I speak, the thin tear in the . . . in the f-fabric of space. That is where Casha is. She was the love of my life, and yet I cannot keep her in f-focus. I cannot . . . it is true . . . I can barely recall her voice. She has left me. Not as in . . . she has left this planet. She has left me as in . . . she has left the dimensions that we know of as . . . as space and time. Do you understand?"

Patti nodded. She watched Professor Gavrushnekov look into her eyes, then down at her lips, and then at her chest.

"The universe . . ." Elena placed her hand on her own neck, then put it down on her other hand, which was still resting on Patti's, "the universe is a . . . it is a vagina. It is a beautiful . . . it is a dark, very large . . . it is a vagina of infinite expanse. Having come to lesbianism late in my life, I have never . . . f-felt . . . I have . . . it has never been . . . the opportunity to f-feel such f-full breasts as yours up against my own . . . to bring the young and the old female form . . . to have young and old star clusters, as it were . . . in space the young stars devour the old ones . . . it is f-fitting and right. It is . . . I am just . . . I am bursting with desire, Miss Tipendorf. It is p-positively shameful."

Elena Gavrushnekov slowly raised her hands up and sent them toward Patti Tipendorf's fantastic breasts, but they touched only air. Before she had extended her arms, Miss Tipendorf had stood up, knocking her chair to the floor. She ran past the coffee bar, through the small crowd of students waiting for espresso drinks, out the doors, onto the sidewalk, and now she crossed Excellence Drive. The wind, which had uncharacteristically not blown for weeks, picked up now, pulling strands of her hair out of her headband and making her eyes tear. Excellence was famous for its winds, which screamed through the fields of corn and soybeans, over dried-up riverbeds and partially shutdown factories, across railroad tracks and the Interstate. You could see, in the creviced and cracked faces of the elderly who had lived in Excellence all their lives, how brutal the wind was over time; how much hardness it required, how much steadfastness, to stare into it day after day. It was the wind that drove the graduates of Excellence University to the coasts, either east or west, it didn't matter, just so long as they were someplace else. It was the wind that swept away each new generation, leaving behind just a handful of stragglers who were, for whatever reason, stuck in the Midwest.

Patti was to meet with Professor Wilkins in the afternoon to discuss the ordering of office supplies. In the quivering smile he had already displayed several times she had glimpsed what Professor Gavrushnekov had described, but how was his behavior any different from what she had just encountered in Fresh Roast? And how was it that different from how the boys acted at fraternity parties around town, or in the bars off the pedestrian mall? Where were the uninterested parties, the people who were supposed to be waiting at college to educate and inspire her? And who was she going to get to write her letters of recommendation? There was, she thought as she crossed the quad, no such thing as ideas. Or, at the very least, there were ideas, but not without people, and people were all the same: young and old, male and female. People just thought about themselves.

Elena sat for several minutes at her table, waiting for Jason to notice that she needed a refill of coffee. She looked down at the papers in front of her, at the pseudo-intellectual musings she had tried to jot down, all in a pathetic attempt to justify this inexhaustible life energy she felt pounding through her debilitated body. It was the secret of all secrets, guarded carefully so that the young would not suspect the truth: the awful, brazen fact that love was itself a biological force, a—what was the phrase in that poem?—a green fuse that drives the flower. And it should be hidden too, not because it made love any less beautiful a thing to feel, but because it made the dead really dead, so dead, so gone from everything else, everything with color and texture and speech. She had told herself, she had told this girl Patti, that she was writing a theory of the universe, but in fact she had just been trying to find a way, any way, to hold the breasts of a young, nubile body against her own, all while her sweet Casha rotted in the ground in the cemetery on the east side of town. As she sipped from the new mug of coffee placed before her, Elena Gavrushnekov felt the familiar, falling feeling that left her momentarily confused and misplaced, and suddenly she was in Moscow, at the ballet with her Aunt Lavanya, watching the beautiful, malnourished girls younger even than she was fling their bodies into the air, and then she was with Dmitri in their backyard, the magnolia tree magically filled with cardinals and her soon-to-be ex-husband saying, just in passing, "Dreams, they are really everything, aren't they? They are themselves a kind of particle," so that she could see quite clearly that he had begun to lose his mind. And then she was back in Fresh Roast, a manila folder sitting in front of her, which she opened to peruse. Patti Tipendorf's résumé. "I must return this to her in the morning," she said loudly to no one. "I shall write her a little . . . a little note and attach it on top of the f-folder, on top of this sheet f-filled with curly writing. Look at how she spelled *Einstein*: with two e's at the end. Imagine! I shall write her a . . . a note and drop by in the morning. I shall write a note and spell his name wrong as well. Why should the young hoard stupidity so? There is so little difference between . . . between us. The difference is between the living and the dead. Everything else is . . . other differences are very, very small."

Girls I Know

Ginger and I careened along Storrow Drive in her black Lexus, on our way to the Brighton Cryobank for Oncologic and Reproductive Donors. Ginger was a shitty driver in ways that I assume most spoiled rich girls are—blithe disregard for others' rights-of-way, refusal to slow down for pedestrians, etc.—but I can't be sure since Ginger is the only spoiled rich girl I've ever known. As she cut off a ComElectric truck I thought of Robert Lowell, the subject of my dissertation, and the time he had Jean Stafford in his father's car and ran into a wall, smashing her nose to bits. "There was about a 25 percent reduction in the aesthetic value of her face," Lowell's friend, Blair Clark, said. A short time later, Lowell asked Stafford to marry him. It was the honorable thing to do, marry the woman whose face he had ruined, and Lowell was nearing the height of his honorable phase, although I don't think he became a worse person necessarily as he grew older. The idea of virtue was always mesmerizing to him, only he could never live up to his ideals for very long. His life was filled with these bold gestures of magnanimity that were always, in the end, withdrawn—not out of insincerity as much as an insufficient attention span. The mania and mad delusions were symptoms, not causes, of his alternating embrace of piety and savageness, at least that's how I understood him back then. I don't think of Lowell that much now, at least not Lowell the person, although I still read his poems fairly regularly.

Shifting gears with her bare feet, her mouth filled with bubble gum, Ginger gave me a sidelong glance. "What you thinking over there, retard?" She dropped the second 'r' out of the last word to imitate a Southie accent, which she did pretty well.

I told her about Lowell's car accident, how he lived—in part—off the royalties of Stafford's first book, *A Boston Adventure*, for several years before openly cheating on her with a visitor to their Maine home, prompting separation and then divorce. "If we got in a car wreck today and I fractured all my vertebrae," I cut to the point, "would you marry me?"

We had been hanging out a lot over the past month or so, ever since she had moved into my building at the end of May and mentioned casually—in response to the bewildering description I offered of my intellectual interests—that her grandfather had known Lowell at Harvard. They had played tennis together a few times, hung out some socially in the Yard, before Lowell decided to transfer to study with John Crowe Ransom and Allen Tate, first at Vanderbilt and then at Kenyon. That made Ginger, so knobby-kneed and awkward, suddenly shimmer in my eyes; she was two degrees separated from a major American poet, even if he had died right before she had been born. Growing up in Burlington, Vermont, the only people my childhood friends were two degrees separated from were French Canadian prostitutes. So my motives for getting to know her were compromised from the beginning, but I don't fault myself for that. I came to Boston to enter Lowell's world as best I could and now—years after basically giving up on that enterprise—Ginger had fallen into my lap.

"I don't think I'd marry you," she said slowly as we rounded a corner, "but my family would help you out financially—you know, redo your kitchen so you could reach all the cabinets from your wheelchair."

"Well, that's definitely something."

She adjusted the volume of one of her Radiohead bootlegs via an inconspicuous button on her steering wheel. "You should be writing on Bishop anyway," she said. "She's the one who grew up with her grandparents, not Lowell."

Early on I had let slip that I had never known my father and that my mother had died when I was eleven of ovarian cancer. Ginger never let go of the information and tried to read it into everything I did, so if I nursed a cup of coffee, or that hideous green tea she was continually brewing, and claimed it was because the beverage was too hot to drink, she'd shake her head knowingly, tap me on the arm and whisper, "detachment anxiety." I had wanted her to see me as transcending my background, even if I didn't believe such a thing was possible. That was the problem with Bishop: writing about someone who came from nowhere, or someplace even farther away than nowhere, Nova Scotia, would have just taken me back again and again to the clapboard house of my grandparents: the three of us playing Parcheesi while a PBS show on the National Park Service droned on in the background and Easter bread baked in the kitchen. So I tried to ignore her poems altogether, even though they spoke to me keenly.

"But I like the Brahmins," I replied that day, using the same hollow justification I always did. "I like their self-indulgence. Bishop, Stevens, Williams, they're all too sincere."

"You're a retard, Walt. Wallace Stevens kicks Lowell's ass, and he was an insurance lawyer. An insurance lawyer! No, Lowell knew he sucked; that's why, when he rewrote his poems, he tried to ruin them."

She baited me like this all the time, which I secretly loved. My retorts were invariably pathetic, though. "His genius was self-consuming . . ." I mumbled.

Every other Wednesday was my drop day at the sperm bank.

If I could persuade her, Ginger would give me a ride, and sometimes after I was done we'd spend the day together, either driving around Boston or trading Lowell lines back and forth over gin gimlets at her place. If she weren't around, I'd take the T out to Brighton by myself, do my drop, then come home and try to work on the dissertation. The premise of "Robert Lowell and the Poetics of Yankee Peerage" was, I had realized with some shame two years before, pathetically simple: Lowell's poetry was shaped by where he chose to live and who his parents were. Although I had been in graduate school in the English Department at B.U. for seven years I had yet to complete a draft of my introduction, not to mention any of the other chapters. The project had long since lost the interest of my advisor, and the poetry world as well seemed to have lost interest in Lowell, although every thin volume of autobiographical lyrics published still owed its shape—I was convinced—to *Life Studies*, published in 1959. Outside of Boston, I learned secondhand from the few graduates of our program who had managed to secure assistant professorships, Lowell was thought to be unteachable. No one cared about the old South Boston Aquarium anymore, and Lowell's pedigree made him deeply suspect in curricula shaped by identity politics—even if he had stood as a conscientious objector to World War II, was in and out of mental wards his entire adult life, and traveled with Eugene McCarthy in his hopeless bid for the Democratic Party's presidential nomination. He had also broken Stafford's nose not just once, in their car accident, but also another time with his bare hand, versified excerpts from the letters of his second wife without her permission, even drowned three kittens given to him by a friend, although this last damning bit of information was never fully substantiated. Ginger was right; Bishop had become the preeminent poet of her generation, if posthumously, which meant that even while I had picked the right city in which to study poetry, I had also managed to pick the wrong poet.

There were faster ways to Brighton than Storrow Drive but that was the route we'd always take. It gave Ginger the opportunity to identify her Harvard classmates to me as they jogged along the Charles, the ones who had opted to spend the summer in Boston, taking over spacious apartments like the one she had sublet on the top floor of the building where I was the super. I'd ask endless questions about her acquaintances and she'd answer as many as she could, knowing how much I hungered for telling details: "Her dad invented antidepressants," she'd say, or, "He's in line for the Dutch throne." Half the time she was probably lying but I gobbled up the morsels she threw my way regardless. It was harder to get Ginger to talk about her own life, but the pace she kept revealed a lot. She was always having to rush to New York for a family obligation, or drive to Mattapoisett for some aunt's anniversary. When she wasn't on the move she'd complain to me about what a boring and dreary summer she was having and how much nicer it would be to have no such encumbrances. "To have nothing to do but masturbate for money and read poetry," she'd say, "that sounds awesome." She never figured out, or at least never acknowledged, how absolutely broke I was, but that was probably her just trying to go easy on me. I so wanted her to see me as viable in some way, even though I was eleven years her senior and half her intelligence.

We turned onto Commonwealth Avenue, drove past those beautiful homes that poke out behind arbors, brick walls, and elm trees, then merged onto North Beacon. I can't remember when I've been happier than right then: in that beautiful car, angst rock blaring on the speakers. Since taking a year off from school to write *Girls I Know*, the book for which she would receive a six-figure advance at the end of that summer, Ginger hasn't phoned me once. That's my fault, though, not hers, which is the odd thing: my self-pity crested that summer but I was the one, at the end of the day, who was bent on hurting others. It serves me right that now I orbit around those images I have of Ginger's self-conscious, endearing beauty, or recall the clever phrases she'd coin without any effort, all while I labored to be witty and edgy in her presence. How odd to think that it was me standing on the precipice that summer even as I did nothing. How odd that the inaugural moment for *Girls I Know* would mark my own entry into that unappreciated demographic of single men who—rather than be invited to the Cape with the young families squirting up like daisies all around—are instead pent in glass and sent floating through Boston to gaze all too surreptitiously on the unknowable gaggles of the city's borrowed beauties.

"What's it like, collecting jiz all day?" Ginger had produced a small, leather-bound notebook I had never seen before from her oversized straw bag while I signed in at the cryobank. The heavy-set black nurse shot Ginger a cold stare before affixing labels to a couple of sample jars and walking around the counter. They had started two-cupping me a few months before, when my sperm count began to drop. Now I had to separate the first shot, in which my sperm concentration was the greatest, from the second. It was not an easy maneuver, not that anyone ever asked.

The nurse led me down the hallway toward one of the small private rooms. "Think of me, darling," Ginger shouted as she began to thumb through a *McCall's* in the waiting room. The donor rooms were filled with porn, but the waiting room didn't push the envelope at all—just your typical pile of outdated magazines, a few condensed books, and some pamphlets on STDs and bulimia.

I never used any of the donor aids; the magazines smelled of unwashed men's hands; the videos were too long and involved and the VCRs were typically broken anyway. I would think of the girl who worked at the convenience store across the street from our building, her pierced eyebrow, the apron she wore smeared with nacho cheese drippings, or that Israeli student I taught at B.U. a few years before with jet black hair and leather everything. I never thought of Ginger.

Just a few months ago, Irena, a woman I know who works at the Victor Hugo Bookshop on Newbury Street, asked about my sperm. I don't know how she had learned about me whoring my DNA, but I had seen her more than once in the back row at the Grolier poetry readings with a woman I assumed was her girlfriend and I figured my part-time job was gossip that had bubbled up at one point. I told her that I was flattered by her interest and she quickly corrected me. "I don't want your seed," she replied, "I just want to know your lot number." It turned out, she explained, that some of the banks had a reputation for lying about the characteristics and backgrounds of their donors. I was intrigued and gave her my information. A week later I saw her in the bookstore, perched back behind that enclosed counter they have, chopsticks sticking out of her hair. "They say you're a six-one Ivy Leaguer with blue eyes," she said. *Was there,* I thought, *nothing of me worth advertising?* "You should be thrilled," she went on, knowing—I inferred later—enough of my intellectual interests to see the irony of it all. "In twenty years, every adopted WASP in Boston will look like you."

After I finished my drop that day we got on the Turnpike and raced back into town. No more meandering along the Charles, Ginger was either in a hurry to catch the shuttle back to New York or just feeling antsy, I wasn't sure which.

"What's with the notebook?" Its corner had poked out of her straw purse, reminding me of its earlier appearance at the sperm bank.

"Idea I have," she shrugged, "for a book."

My eyebrows arched.

"It'll be called *Girls I Know* and will be comprised of interviews I'll do with women from all walks of life: secretaries, custodians, lawyers, strippers, women who collect ejaculates at sperm banks—"

"Is that a word, 'ejaculates'?"

"I think so."

I shifted in the leather seat. "Did she talk to you, that woman, after your line about jiz?"

"She warmed up to me when I told her about the book project. Women like it when other women write down what they say."

"Is that right." I was feeling crabby suddenly, I wasn't sure why.

"She says it's a good job. They have really great benefits. She said lots of times the men can't produce their first time in. Did you have any problems?"

"No." We drove by a group of daycare kids walking in twos, holding onto a rope. "When did we start treating our young like cattle?" I wondered aloud.

"We love our children too much," she said. "We gag them with the idea of childhood as idyllic. 'Hold on to this rope and you'll be just fine.' It's ridiculous."

I loved it when she generalized facilely from her Upper East Side upbringing. She pulled behind the building, into her reserved parking place, and we got out.

It was Ginger's book concept that had changed my mood; *Girls I Know* had begun to work on me, at first I wasn't sure why.

"How'd you come up with the idea for your book?" I asked.

"I want to write something without my own voice," she said. "I want to get out of myself."

"Don't we all," I replied, but I was kidding myself, I realize now. At the time I assumed that I was just as self-loathing as the next guy, or girl, but what I took to be self-evisceration back then was really just an artistic form of narcissism that characterized all the poems to which I found myself drawn. I was reading the same thing over and over again, and when I didn't find what I was looking for I projected it. Every poem was about the need to register one's self-disgust. Every poem was written with me in mind.

We walked into the building and she pushed the button for the elevator.

"Do you want to take a nap or something, after expending yourself?"

"No, I'm not tired."

We waited for the doors to open, then stepped inside the car. In her own at once vulnerable and sassy way, Ginger had been trying to seduce me for weeks, but I had resisted, mainly because I couldn't understand her attraction to me and thought—admittedly in a paranoid way—that if our bodies ever coupled she would never have anything to do with me again and I would lose my glimpse into American aristocracy once and for all. After rejecting her for the third time the week before, she had refrained from asking me up since, but that day I didn't really ask for an invitation; I just tagged along.

Although the apartment she was subletting from a family friend was a fully furnished two bedroom, Ginger had pitched her camp in the living room. Her white futon was on the floor, her trunk open next to it, with expensive clothes piled around it, partially covering an enormous boom box and a bunch of worn paperbacks—books by Hans Küng, Sylvia Plath, and Cormac McCarthy. There were also snake droppings on the floor, left by her pet python, Sid, and the lingering odor of green curry, which she put in everything she cooked.

We sat on the edge of the futon, our feet touching, and began to kiss. I placed my hand on her nub of a breast and she leaned back but I didn't follow her lead. She stared up at the ceiling for a moment, then asked if I wanted some warm tap water and walked into the kitchen. "'When you left,'" I called to her as she walked out, "'I thought of you each hour of the day.'" "'Each minute of the hour, each second of the minute,'" she hollered back. It was remarkable; after a single measly poetry survey course, Ginger had somehow managed to commit a whole pile of Lowell lines to memory. She came back in with Sid wrapped around her neck, having forgotten about the water. I was actually relieved to see the snake, hoping he'd give us something to talk about so that we wouldn't have to address why I was leading Ginger on and then pulling back.

"Look," she whispered to her pet, her fingers tickling his skin a few inches below his mouth, "it's the superintendent of the building, here to enforce the 'No Pets' rule and take you away." She held him out toward me.

"I, uh . . . that's okay." I didn't like to touch Sid; he scared the hell out of me. What's more, I knew—at the end of the summer—that I'd be the one scraping python shit off the floor. Ginger sat down a good three feet away from me, depositing her pet between us. He curled around her and slithered back into the kitchen.

I looked over at her, at her torn and patched denim cutoffs, the Green Day tee shirt off of which she had ripped the neckband. In a moment I was lost in one of those reveries that constantly sucked me in that summer: the two of us living in one of her family's seven vacation homes, dividend checks piled on Louis XIV dressers, my dog-eared copies of Lowell replaced with first editions. Through a staggering manipulation of connections, a professorship at Brown University had been secured for me. On the weekends we boated off Martha's Vineyard.

"I want a Twinkie," she said. I nodded my head eagerly, she grabbed her purse, and we left.

The first day of her residency in my building, just a few scant hours after she had revealed her connection to Lowell while supervising the professional movers she had hired to drive a barely filled van one-and-a-half miles from Harvard Square to the corner of Beacon and Mass Ave, I visited Ginger in her sublet. It had been my intention to leave her alone for a full day but I couldn't stop myself. In addition to her trunk, she had two enormous duffel bags, neither of which she would ever fully unpack, their unzipped tops disgorging clothes as if alive. In one of the bags, under a pair of silk pajamas, I thought I made out the hull of a vibrator. In another were piles of letters, bound with string, written—I would discover much later—by her grandmother, who, before dying of liver cancer, suffered from insomnia and wrote Ginger every night for three-and-a-half years, mostly to complain of the infidelities of her long-dead husband and rail against the inadequate disposal of our nation's spent nuclear reactor rods, apparently her one current-events obsession.

Ginger watched me look over her belongings without making small talk. I asked her about the classes she had taken the previous year. "I don't remember the course titles," she said, "just the stuff we read."

"Well," I tried again, "what did you read?"

"In one class we read Aquinas. I remember his ontological proof for the existence of God: 'But as soon as the signification of the name *God* is understood, it is at once seen that God exists. For by this name is signified that thing than which nothing greater can be conceived. But that which exists actually and mentally is greater than that which exists only mentally. Therefore, since as soon as the name *God* is understood it exists mentally, it also follows that it exists actually. Therefore the proposition *God exists* is self-evident.'"

"Do all of your friends have photographic memories?"

She wrinkled her mouth. "I don't know. I don't have friends. I have acquaintances, classmates, cousins." She sat down on the floor, having yet to unfurl her futon. "In another class we read Faulkner. All I remember is Cash's line about Darl at the very end of *As I Lay Dying*: 'This world is not his world; this life his life.'"

I just smiled. I had never read a word of Faulkner—still haven't.

"I read Roethke in the same class that had some Lowell in it. Do you know 'I Knew a Woman'? 'These old bones live to learn her wanton ways.'"

"'I measure time by how a body sways.'"

"I like his poems more than Lowell's."

"Roethke!"

She smiled with her head bent down so that her eyes had to roll up in their sockets to look at me.

"Did your grandfather," I figured it was fair game now, since she had mentioned him before, "did he by chance remain friends with Lowell after he left Harvard?" I was on the hunt for an unknown correspondence, perhaps a letter or two that hadn't been picked over by other scholars.

"Nope. Sorry." She noticed me looking down at her own collection of yellowing envelopes and added, "No one in my family ever wrote, or received a letter from, Lowell. I don't think Grandfather liked him very much—something about his temper."

"He didn't have his first manic attack," here I had the opportunity to defend the patrician poet against his patrician detractor and I took it up eagerly, "until he was about thirty-two. But he was violent, even as a child. He beat up kids all the time at St. Mark's, punched his father out. That's why everyone called him Cal, for Caliban, or Caligula."

She didn't try to reclaim the conversation; she just let me go on for a while. I peppered her with a sampling of my Lowell anecdotes: him climbing up on a statue naked while in Argentina during a breakdown, getting lost in Caroline Blackwood's mansion the night before he died, refusing President Lyndon Johnson's invitation to read at the White House. She seemed neither entirely interested in what I had to say nor altogether bored.

"Do you ever feel so cramped in your own skin," she asked when I had exhausted myself, "that you'd do anything to crawl out? Do you ever look in the mirror and just want to erase your face?"

I paused, not sure how to respond.

"I think it's a girl thing," she added, "wanting to make yourself disappear. Boys think of shooting people; girls think of starvation."

After eating Twinkies and drinking Mountain Dew at the convenience store across the street from our building, Ginger decided to begin her research for *Girls I Know* and I tagged along. We went to the Glass Slipper. It's nice, entering a strip club with a young girl. The enormous black bouncer gave me a knowing nod and we were quickly ushered to a choice booth right in front just as the next dancer came down the staircase and onto the stage. The DJ situated in a booth on our left began to spin some techno music but the speakers were blown and the sound came out muffled. As my eyes adjusted to the half-light I noticed that the place was basically deserted. The stripper had on a business suit that was about two sizes too small and was holding a briefcase that she set down in the middle of the stage while looking menacingly at Ginger, her tongue heavy on her lower lip.

"Her tits are busting out," Ginger said. "I wish my tits busted out." She took out her notebook, looked around the place a little bit, then began to scribble furiously.

"It's the people who don't have any reason to give a shit that do things with their lives," I said, watching her write. "Why is that?"

She held up an index finger, finished her thought, then shut her book. "I don't know," she said in response, waving at one of the waitresses. "Maybe it's just easier than doing nothing."

I had been trying, roughly since Ginger was in middle school, to do something other than nothing, to get my PhD, and I wasn't finding it easy at all. A thin waitress in fishnet stockings and a strapless tank top sauntered over. She had dirty black hair tied off in a ponytail, dark eye shadow, and lipstick.

"What can I get you?" Like everyone else in the place, she looked at Ginger, not me.

"I'm writing a book about women," Ginger said, sliding over toward me and nodding at the space next to her. "Tell me your story."

The woman looked over her shoulder, then over at me. "You want something to drink?"

"Bud."

She nodded and looked at Ginger, who ordered a gin gimlet.

When the waitress walked away I knocked Ginger with my

elbow to tease her about being shut down but she ignored me. On stage, the stripper had opened her briefcase and taken out an enormous dildo that she waved at us like a handgun. Ginger pointed up at the ceiling, where there were mirrors I hadn't noticed. The dancer walked up the stairs, then came back down minus the suit and dildo, in a black teddy. She put her arms around the pole in the middle of the stage and began to buck and twist, the lingerie slipping to the ground. Looking at the woman's back as it was reflected off the mirrors behind the stage, I noticed a purple stain on her skin.

"Birthmark?" I asked Ginger.

"I'm thinking more burn than birth." She nodded her head authoritatively. We both looked at it for a few seconds. "It's shaped like Rhode Island," she added.

The waitress came back with our drinks. She asked me for nine dollars. I pointed at Ginger, who gave her twenty.

"So you're writing a book?"

Ginger nodded. "*Girls I Know.*"

"Sheila," the woman nodded at another waitress, "can you get a scotch and soda for the guy at eight?"

I couldn't see Sheila's reaction but I did watch as the waitress set her tray down on our table and squeezed in next to Ginger. After the stripper in front of us had crawled over to pick a twenty out of Ginger's hand with her mouth, she told us about her life.

"I ran away from home at thirteen," she began. "We were living with my mom's boyfriend in Rumford, Maine, a piece of shit town. I don't remember the guy's name. He had two kids. One of them was mental—really big and strong but would spit up his food and crap on himself. The other went to juvenile hall cuz he kept on trying to rape the girls in his homeroom. He was a year older than me.

"Mom was diabetic and didn't work. She got disability money because her left eye was no good. The guy she was with then was real fat. He didn't work neither. The two of them would sit around, drink, and watch TV. Whenever I was alone with him, he would smile at me in a fucked-up way. He never touched me, though. I heard them talking about it one night and my mom was like, 'if you want it so bad go give it a try, just don't hurt her,' so I left.

"It wasn't like I meant to run away for good. I was really just planning on walking around. I went into a grocery store and decided I was going to buy some cigarettes only I didn't have any money, so I swiped a pack and then out in the parking lot this guy came up to me and said he had seen what I had done with the Marlboro Lights and he was going to turn me in. I begged him not to, I actually thought he could get me into trouble, and he said he wouldn't but that I should get home and he'd give me a ride. So I got in his car with him.

"He took me to his house all the way up near Oquossoc, me screaming the whole way, pounding on the window. No one in any of the cars we passed looked over at us. When we got to his place he locked me in his basement. A couple times a day he'd give me food. There was a sink and shower down there. I'd go to the bathroom in the sink. A few days later he came downstairs with a mattress and another man. The man gave him money to rape me. I don't know how much. I found out later that the guy had taken out ads in porn magazines. 'Young Girl Who Likes Pain.' It took me a month of getting the shit raped out of me to figure out a way out of there. I ended up knocking the door down with a section of pipe when he was gone one day.

"I didn't feel like I could go home after that so I moved to Waterville, then Berlin, New Hampshire, then Manchester. I did tricks, worked in a convenience store for a while. I didn't look like I was thirteen no more. I got arrested for stuff, nothing serious, mostly just cuz I had nowhere to go. Then I started doing speed and LSD and other shit guys would give me to fuck them or suck them off. I'm eighteen now. I take Concord Trailways down from Manchester on Monday and waitress and dance here through Wednesday. I can't dance on the weekends because they say my tits aren't big enough and I can't afford no enlargements. So I work and buy my shit down here for the week. One of my girlfriends looks after my boy while I'm gone in exchange for speed. I had him two years ago, Jayce. I work down here so it won't ever get back to him, how I make money."

A guy sitting a few tables away gave her a wave and she stood up, picked up her tray, and went back to work. As she walked off, I couldn't bear to look at Ginger. She had started scribbling notes again and I didn't want her to read my face. I was thinking that she might end up with a pretty good book.

When we got outside, we found broken glass all over the sidewalk on the passenger side of the Lexus. Someone had taken a crowbar to her dashboard in an attempt to swipe her disc player but had only gotten it halfway out. "At least finish the job," she said, surveying the damage.

An older man walked out of an adult bookstore across the street. "Is that your car?" Ginger nodded. "The alarm's been howling for the last twenty minutes. It just stopped."

She looked at him. "That's what alarms do, they howl."

He walked away while I tried to use one of my Birkenstock clogs to brush the broken glass off the front seats. It didn't work too well. We got in and took off.

Ginger drove through the city streets just as she did on Storrow Drive, carelessly aggressive. It wasn't rush hour yet but there were lots of pedestrians walking around and I stared at them, wondering what they were thinking, how it must have felt to have to get dressed up every day for work—exhausting, but then again you've got money in the bank at the end of the month and that doesn't sound all bad. I glanced over and noticed she was smiling. Ginger had three kinds of smiles: there was one that wasn't really a smile but a smirk, which she used when needling me about Lowell, another one that was a smile on the outside only, eyes vacant, kind of a social mask she had probably developed just to simplify her family encounters. The third smile was a girlish grin; it was my favorite one—very rare, but also very sweet. That was the one I glimpsed for a moment right then.

"What?" I asked her.

She shook her head.

"No, what?"

She shrugged. "I can feel shards of glass in my ass."

"Me too." We laughed.

She turned onto Mass Ave. In a few minutes we'd be home. I'd be listening to the phone messages left by tenants who needed their toilets fixed; I'd be wondering how to avoid my dissertation on my own.

"'We're knotted together in innocence and guile,'" she said. Remarkably, she had settled on my favorite of all of Lowell's sonnets.

"'Yet we are not equal.'" I replied. I didn't say the rest of the line, not right then. We sat at a light that didn't want to change. Finally she turned to me.

"You know, Walt, it's not my fault that I have the background I do."

I was barely listening. The ingenuously simple premise of *Girls I Know* had reasserted itself in my mind and, horrifically, I found myself comparing it to my hieroglyphic of a dissertation, with envisioned chapters on Lowell and Boston infrastructure, the discernible metrical cadence of lithium, and an allegorical reading of "Sailing Home from Rapallo" as an anticolonial critique of French Symbolic Poetry. I thought of Ginger on the shuttle to New York, headed back for a weekend filled with parties, or having lunch with one of her professors at the Harvard Faculty Club, or just applying to Harvard in the first place. Had she even bothered to write a personal statement, or did people with last names like hers skip that step? And I thought of my grandfather up in Burlington, probably at that moment attempting once more to make it through some of Lowell's verse so that he could talk to me about my work, ask pertinent questions—try to be my father.

Now, in hindsight, I see it differently; I see, in her clumsy self-defense, one last attempt to reach out across the distance that I insisted existed between us, a distance made up of privilege and want that I felt—like some key to all mythologies—could explain every person or poem I encountered. Now I see her trying to become my friend.

"Yes it is," I said.

After reading poems from *Life Studies* that he sent her as he put the collection together, Elizabeth Bishop wrote Lowell a letter about what it felt like for her to see him write about his illustrious family. "I am green with envy of your kind of assurance," she said. "I feel that I could write in as much detail about my Uncle Artie, say—but what would be the significance? Nothing at all." She had an uncle, like everyone, but Lowell had something different, his genealogy. "All you have to do," she went on, "is put down the names!"

It has to be the most exasperated she ever sounded, at least on paper, but Bishop got over it; she continued to write her own kind of poems, and kept up her friendship with Lowell until the day he died. When he moved to England, Bishop took his place at Harvard, teaching poetry to kids like Ginger. He had so much acclaim in his life, she had some but not as much. When Lowell was playing as a boy on Revere Street in Boston, Bishop was up in Nova Scotia, watching her grandparents grow older still. Where is her bitterness? It must be somewhere in her work and yet I can't seem to find it. For a time she seemed to consider wrecking herself—becoming an alcoholic, writing nothing at all—but she didn't. She went on in her quiet, quizzical way. I don't see how she did it.

"I have lived without sense so long the loss no longer hurts." That's the next line in the sonnet Ginger started to speak in her car that day. Like I said, it's a great poem.

———

There were other days we spent together after that one but not many. Ginger began to avoid me. I, as a result, started to pine for her—copying poems and leaving them on her door, even assembling a pyramid of Twinkies on her "Welcome" mat late one night. She didn't tell me about her advance until the day she moved out, when her parents sent up their driver to take her stuff not over the Harvard Bridge and back into Cambridge but rather down to New York. "I'm going to write my book, I thought it might be easier in the city," she said with a shrug. I had to pry the monetary amount out of her by guessing incrementally larger dollar figures. When she pulled away it occurred to me that I had never seen Ginger with anyone other than me since I had met her—that maybe those acquaintances of hers that jogged every afternoon along the Charles were just that, acquaintances, and that her summer had probably been a lonely one, even with all the engagements.

In the past year I haven't gone anywhere; I'm still the super at the same building, although my dissertation has been redesignated in my mind as no longer stalled but abandoned. Generational shifts occur in Boston every four years; you last through one cycle of college students and suddenly you're on the inside of the outside, as close as you'll ever get to being *from* here, even if you grew up in a New England outpost, rooting for the Red Sox like everyone else. It's been almost a decade for me but I finally feel settled into life here, if in a permanently qualified way.

On the T yesterday I thought of those of us who migrated here for ridiculous reasons, because of a few lines of poetry, those of us whom the city has permitted to burrow into its hide even though we have nothing to offer, and I imagined, years down the road, when my artificially inseminated sons have grown into boys, stepping onto the Red Line and suddenly finding myself surrounded by my likenesses. They might be slightly different shades of me, maybe different features here and there, but I will recognize them as my own, all squeezed together for a chance stop or two, reading their library books or just gazing out the window, oblivious to the presence of their father, the man who provided them with their ghostly parentage: with the unknowable lines of a peculiar, faint family.

Labor
Day
Hurricane,
1935

I'll tell you everything I remember from those days, although surely I have rearranged certain details, or forgotten others altogether. What I do remember I feel as if I can reach out and touch, but what I can't recall has slipped away from me for good. That's the greatest effect that aging has had on me: not that I forget things, but that what I remember I *really* remember. The memories that haven't dissolved have hardened and calcified inside of me, like so many of my body's infirmities.

I remember very little about the hurricane itself, in part because it hit the Middle Keys, not the Lower, so we were spared the brunt of its power. Unlike others, even others in my family,

I was not surprised when the storm arrived because my Uncle Archibald had predicted its appearance early Sunday afternoon, almost exactly twenty-four hours in advance. Uncle Archibald had a barometer on his front porch that he checked with religious regularity during the summer and early fall. When the barometer's mercury went down, however slightly, he would relate the news to one of my three brothers. They, especially Jerry and Jack, were almost always out front, either doing yard work or chatting with friends. I was not privy to Uncle Archibald's summonings, as I was usually inside, doing the housework with my mother, sewing, reading, or helping Frederick with his piano scales. As a young girl I had spent hours every day playing in our lush, overgrown yard—chasing lizards with Jerry and Jack, or playing hide-and-seek with Frederick once he was old enough—but in 1935 I was sixteen and young women did not play outside with their brothers back then. Rather, they helped their mothers keep house, or minded their younger siblings.

I adored all of my brothers, each for slightly different reasons. Like our father, Jerry and Jack were lean and tall, with fair, ruddy complexions, and thin, sandy hair. While we had always been close growing up, by that summer it was clear that they inhabited a new world of which I could only sneak glimpses; now there were moments when they lowered their voices when I entered the room, or shared a laugh over an unspecified adventure in which I had played no part. Jerry was the oldest, at nineteen, but it was Jack, two years younger, who was the most serious and—I suppose—most like our father, although he tempered his naturally stern expression with a wry smile you had to be looking for to catch. Frederick, only eleven, was already of a stockier build than his brothers, with dark hair like our mother's and dazzling, green eyes. He was liable to do anything, from dragging a half-dead water rat into the house to throwing coconuts onto our tin roof from the palm tree in back, convincing my mother that we were being attacked by the German soldiers who were rumored to be setting up camps in Mexico. Frederick was incorrigible but also sweet, and we all awaited his adolescence and young adulthood with a mix of excitement and dread.

Perhaps because I was given relatively few opportunities to stare into its glass up close, I believed fully in the talismanic powers of Uncle Archibald's barometer. He had ordered the device out of the Sears Roebuck Catalogue four years before and had paid a princely sum for it to be shipped, in a crate packed with straw, down to Key West. Its glass tube was set in a thick iron stand that stood to the immediate right of his front door, where others on the island placed umbrella holders. Its prominent positioning had rankled my mother when it was first unveiled. "Is it absolutely necessary," she had asked my father at dinner, "for your brother to adorn the front of his home with scientific experiments?" This was in 1931, when Mother still spoke at dinner. My father did not bother to answer her and she never brought it up again.

That Sunday, just minutes after our lunch was concluded, Uncle Archibald had been so bold as to come over and speak to my father directly, telling him through the open window on the front porch that a hurricane of ferocious proportions was brewing in the Florida Straits.

"I know of its ferocity," he added, his fingers flicking the ends of his moustache, "because of the precipitous drop of the mercury in the barometer. You see, rather than flutter as it has in the past, atmospheric pressure is now falling steadily. It's already below twenty-eight, a very bad sign indeed."

But my father dismissed the dire warning, as he always did, with a wave of his hand, and Uncle Archibald doffed his straw hat and shuffled back to his house without another word. Like the rest of us, he was accustomed to our father's grim, ruthless ways, but Uncle Archibald seemed scarcely perturbed by it, or anything else, save the readings he made of barometric pressure in our vicinity.

In the late summer and early fall, Uncle Archibald announced the annihilation of Key West on a daily basis. It was never the case that a storm might graze the tip of the island, or churn up the water on the Atlantic side. Rather, Uncle Archibald interpreted every fluctuation in his barometer with hopeful fatalism as a sign that we were soon going to be left floating in Garrison Bight, holding onto the thick, slatted shutters of our homes. Uncle Archibald was obsessed with instruments of measurement in general. In the dark wood sitting room of his home was a wicker rocking chair, dozens of milk crates filled with bicycle parts, piles of botany and horticultural books, several antique thermometers, a thermoscope handcrafted in Italy, supposedly according to designs left by Galileo, a large ship compass said to have been retrieved from the USS *Maine*, and a mammoth portrait of Theodore Roosevelt. Uncle Archibald adored the former president, although, like my father, he cared little for the current one, FDR. In fact, Uncle Archibald went so far as to model his handlebar moustache loosely on the Rough Rider's facial hair, refusing to cut it off even after it had been out of style for more than a decade. He even tried to add sizable girth to his frame, but no one in our family, save Uncle Edwin, seemed capable of putting on any weight and so Uncle Archibald remained his gaunt self. He always had a freshly cut hibiscus in the lapel of his faded seersucker jacket, or some other flower that had often been grafted with another species of plant, so that the petals were curiously shaped and the color otherworldly. The right pocket of his jacket seemed to fill on its own with saltwater taffy that could otherwise only be purchased in Miami for an outrageous sum, so that when any of us children greeted him we usually dipped our hand into the pocket ourselves, unless our father was nearby, as he disapproved of such behavior.

More generally, my father disapproved of Uncle Archibald. In the early evenings, he would usually offer his meteorological hunches and my father would wipe them away with the back of his hand. Then he would retire to our back porch for his glass of scotch and a cigar. Uncle Archibald never joined him because he was never invited to, although he made a point of taking a drink and having a smoke on the back porch of *his* house, which was separated from ours by about five feet, at the exact same time. There the two of them would sit, their heads encircled by their respective plumes of cigar smoke, and say nothing. Uncle Archibald might shift loudly in his chair, clear his throat, or slap at a mosquito on his neck or arm while exclaiming for effect, but my father would respond to none of his gesticulations, and the few times that I heard Uncle Archibald dare to ask his older brother a question it went unanswered. While the front porches of our homes, which faced the busy Division Street, required civility, our backyards were enclosed, private, and therefore unencumbered by social niceties.

The source of the tension between the two men was traceable to our family business, Columbia Laundry Service, which my father ran with the aid of his youngest brother, Edwin. Uncle Edwin lived on the other side of the island, considered less fashionable because of the salt ponds and the Catholic churches whose congregations were comprised of the Cubans who had worked in the cigar and pineapple canning factories on Duval Street before the Great Depression came along and wiped them out. Now the men stood in small groups downtown during the day, sharing spirits cloaked in brown bags and occasionally getting in fights. The Atlantic side of Key West was supposedly cooler than the Gulf side due to the trade winds, although neither I nor any of my brothers had ever felt their effects. These winds were supposed to bring some relief to my Aunt Grace, who suffered from asthma and rheumatism, and perhaps they did, but nothing could change the fact that she was married to Uncle Edwin, who was preternaturally irritable and a disturbingly voracious eater of stone crab, which he procured in bulk from a fisherman up on Big Pine Key.

Up until 1929, Uncle Archibald had run the laundry service with Uncle Edwin and my father, but that year, a disagreement ensued that rearranged our family for good. I learned of its particulars only by chance. I was doing the dishes in the kitchen by myself one night because Frederick had fallen out of the ficus tree in back while attempting to imitate one of the neighborhood cats and had required hot compresses that my mother could apply only if Jerry and Jack held down his arms and legs. Exactly what I overheard spoken between Uncle Archibald and Father on our back porch has long since escaped me. The gist was an accusation on Uncle Archibald's part that Uncle Edwin's receipts did not accurately reflect the income of Columbia Laundry Service. While Uncle Archibald, a certified public accountant, balanced the books, it was Edwin who worked the storefront and managed the employees, while my father met with, and tried to solicit, commercial clients for our services. Faced with the choice of regarding either his youngest brother as a thief or his middle brother as a liar, my father opted for the latter, relieving Uncle Archibald of his responsibilities at the store. The consequences of his accusation were probably fully anticipated by Uncle Archibald, who had long ago become too restless to "account" for more than a few hours a day and could usually be found either at the docks downtown, asking fishermen questions about clouds and swells that made their eyebrows wrinkle in confusion, or at the automotive repair shop on Simonton, picking through tires and metal frames that might be used in the construction of a water bicycle he was designing that would make it possible for a single person, with adequate leg strength, to pedal from Key West to Havana.

It was not long after his departure from the family business that it became clear even to us children that Uncle Archibald was up to something more entrepreneurial than the construction of a water bike. First he purchased a new boat: a diesel-powered Tony Jensen, the precise dimensions of which I cannot recall but it must have been at least thirty feet from bow to stern. Uncle Archibald had the wooden hull painted red and named the boat the *Edith Kermit* after Teddy Roosevelt's second wife, implying that he too was starting over again. Why Uncle Archibald needed a boat of such size was a mystery to all of us, until he began to wear so-called Cuban shirts, short-sleeved knits with wide collars and pronounced hems, and smoke Monte Cristos rather than cigars from Tampa. I don't know how we all came to learn that he was using his new vessel to run rum in from Havana, but it was even easier to intuit that his venture was only a partial success. Prohibition ended officially in 1933, but unofficially in Key West sometime before that. There was, quite clearly, more competition in offering spirits on the island than laundering services, and it was not long before Uncle Archibald returned to more conventional dress, although never to Columbia Laundry Service.

Regardless of the situation at the family business, Uncle Archibald was hardly banished from our lives; on the contrary, the more distance created between him and our father, the more appealing he became to me and my brothers. Unlike our father, whose relationship with his middle brother was distanced but still a relationship, Uncle Edwin stopped speaking to Uncle Archibald altogether. Meanwhile, the Great Depression continued to take away our customers, so that by 1935 our paying clients were reduced to two: the Casa Marina Hotel, which needed fewer and fewer sheets and towels to be washed since vacationers in the Keys had slowed to a trickle, and the Florida East Coast Railway. Father had secured this last client in the early 1920s by agreeing to buy all of the linens, towels, napkins, and tablecloths for one of the two trains that would run from Miami to Key West and then leasing their use to the railway on a month-to-month basis. He had borrowed heavily to make the investment but without the outlay we would have never secured the contract and by 1935 it was this contract that kept our laundry service, and by extension our family, afloat when so many businesses and people around us were losing everything.

But I am forgetting the hurricane. Sunday afternoons were solemn times around our house. We would sit together in the living room, dressed in our church clothes, pursuing the silent diversions we were permitted on the Sabbath. Mom usually sat with an open Bible on her lap while Jerry and Jack played a version of checkers that only they understood. I would usually take Frederick under my wing, either to work a puzzle with him or read a book, although that day I cannot recall how he occupied himself. I was sitting on the couch next to Mother, that I do remember, rereading my favorite novel, *Look Homeward, Angel,* when the phone let out a shrill ring.

I'm not sure that our phone had ever rung before on a Sunday, and the occurrence was so odd that my father seemed for the first time that I could remember genuinely unsure what to do. This terrified us all, since that meant he might very well lose his temper and scold us roundly for somehow being responsible for the interruption, which would have reduced our mother to tears. She had been diagnosed as "nervous" just three months before, when she began to cry one afternoon and could not stop, requiring Dr. Moore to come by and prescribe a tablespoon of Dover's powder to be taken with a half glass of brandy before bed each night. A visit to a sanatorium was also proposed, but in the midst of the Depression it was an expense our family could not afford. So it was, I think, in light of her condition that, rather than rage, my father walked over to the kitchen doorway, lifted up the earpiece, and calmly—although sternly—identified himself.

He turned his back to us promptly and spoke for several minutes, much longer than he normally would have, issuing *Yes, sirs* and *Yes, of courses* that were so out of character we all watched with mute fascination. When he hung up he stepped toward us, his hands linked behind his back, and leaned out over his patent-leather shoes, which he stared down at intensely. He was the tallest of his brothers, although by today's standards I suppose his height would be barely average, and he wore his thin, red hair in a severe part that began just above his left ear and veered sharply back over his head. The pink pouches of skin beneath his eyes puckered out above his cheekbones but otherwise his was a body and face filled with sharp edges and straight lines.

"That was Mr. Pinder from the Railway Office in Miami," he said. "The Associated Press has issued a bulletin predicting that a storm, perhaps of hurricane strength, will hit Havana and then pass out into the Gulf sometime tomorrow."

My first impulse was to smile at the news, since it vindicated Uncle Archibald's prediction, at least partly, but I restrained myself.

"To err on the side of caution, however," Father continued, "a rescue train is being sent down to Lower Matecumbe to fetch the men working on the Overseas Highway. It is the train that carries our goods on it, which means that we will have a full load to wash come Tuesday, when regular train service begins again."

None of us said anything. We knew of the workers who were building the highway; they had been Bonus Marchers, World War I veterans who had descended on Washington demanding to be compensated for their service. Franklin Roosevelt had put them to work in the Keys, building a highway that was to run mostly alongside the railway, so that motorists could drive from Miami to Key West without having to take any ferries. Father was opposed to the project, as it would presumably decrease railway traffic and thus our laundry business, and his opposition grew once the highway workers began to flock to Key West on the weekends after their paydays, to drink their wages at the saloons downtown. Jerry, Jack, and their friends had been accosted by these men more than once; they were, in my father's words, a debauched and licentious crew, and the WPA that paid their wages—indeed the whole New Deal—was, according to him, the sign of the end of free enterprise in America.

"Mr. Pinder emphasized," Father continued, "that we should take all due precautions, as this storm might easily veer off its projected path. We shall therefore prepare ourselves for the possible eventuality of being visited directly by this hurricane. Jerry, you and Jack must change into your work clothes, withdraw the storm boards from beneath the front porch, and begin to cover up the windows. Frederick, you may assist them, but only if you promise to be helpful and do as they say." Frederick nodded his head seriously. Father turned to me. "Mary, you and your mother should prepare the interior of the house: take the china out of the cupboards in the kitchen and fill the large pitcher with water from the cistern. We shall ride out the storm in the pantry. I shall go this minute and fetch Uncle Edwin and Aunt Grace, who should not be left alone on the far side of the island when the threat of a serious storm is in the vicinity."

He turned to leave out the back porch but quickly spun around, his thumb hooking into the lower right pocket of his vest, just beneath the chain of his gold watch, as if to thwart his momentum in the other direction. "When you're done with our house, boys," he added, "see to it that Uncle Archibald has his home secured as well. And make it known to him, Jerry, that he is welcome in our home, as I am sure his own pantry is too cluttered to permit him safe refuge. I am also of the opinion, you may convey to him, that there is some safety in numbers."

The boys had already hopped to their feet with excitement, having been spared hours of listless boredom with the prospect of an outdoor activity that our father wouldn't dare interrupt until it was completed. Mother's reaction to our father's speech was more subdued. She placed her open Bible against her chest, closed her eyes for a moment, and placed her hand across the bridge of her nose. She was of slight build and small, almost birdlike, with remarkably pale skin and very thin, black hair that she kept pinned in a bun and, whenever she ventured outside, tucked beneath either one of her feathered hats or a bonnet. Finally she rose to her feet and, without a word, motioned to me. I felt my spirits dip. Since her nervous episode, Mother had barely spoken at all, and her eyes, which were big and black and seemed to occupy a disproportionate amount of her face, shifted nervously, avoiding the gaze of others. Being alone with her, rather than outside with my brothers, was torture, but of course I had no choice in the matter and so I followed her into the kitchen.

We did not learn that the hurricane's path had shifted until later that afternoon, when Mr. Pinder phoned again, this time to report that the storm might hit anywhere between Key West and Key Largo the following day. That evening, we enjoyed a crystal clear sky, a steady, pleasant breeze, and a beautiful sunset. Aunt Grace and Uncle Edwin spent the night in Jerry and Jack's room, which meant that my older brothers slept downstairs: Jack on the daybed in the living room and Jerry on the front porch. There had been little contact between us children and our uncle and aunt, just a dinner marked by the soft clank of silverware against plates and the satisfied grunts of Uncle Edwin. In the morning, we had a small breakfast of Cuban bread and grapefruit. With no chores to do, Jerry, Jack, Frederick, and I were allowed to linger in front of our boarded-up house, in part because my parents were eager to create some distance between us and Aunt Grace, whose lungs were taxed by loud noises and anything else having to do with young people. She had instructed Uncle Edwin to place a chair in the back room behind the kitchen and sat there in seclusion, occasionally calling out to my mother for a fresh glass of limeade.

The four of us stood outside, with strict instructions to stay nearby, and waited for some sign of impending doom. We were all frightened. Key West seemed quieter than usual, even quieter than it typically was on a holiday. No automobiles passed in front of our house, which like the other homes on our street looked alien and bleak. All of the residences were encased in boards and, in some cases, old sails and strips of newspaper, anything to dampen the effect of the expected winds. Bayview Park, which our front porch faced, was utterly deserted, but neither that nor the lack of people about fully explained the calm. It was Jack who noticed that there were no birds on the island; they had all flown away in anticipation of the storm.

Then we saw the band of dark clouds, and felt the first bit of rain, thick drops that fell first haphazardly and then, only a moment later, in sheets. It was just a little after one in the afternoon. Perhaps my memory has played tricks on me, but I seem to recall the entire sky turning black in seconds. My father called to us and as we scurried around to the back of the house I distinctly remember a gust of wind knocking Frederick to his knees. Uncle Archibald rushed over from his back porch just as we rounded the corner of our house, his barometer held awkwardly in his hands, his straw hat pinched under his arm. He had not wanted to venture inside without us, I felt quite sure, and so I gave him a smile meant to be supportive. He responded by wiggling his moustache slightly, wrinkling his eyebrows, and—once we were inside—removing the red royal poinciana blossom from the lapel of his worn, white suit and placing it very gently in my hair above my ear.

Mother and I had set blankets and pillows from the upstairs bedrooms on the floor in the pantry, and the nine of us sat down, with father securing the door behind us. Aunt Grace and Uncle Edwin established themselves at the far end of the cramped room, which was lit by the candelabra from the dining room table. Like our mother, Aunt Grace was dressed in a black satin dress, although she wore a black bonnet low over her face. All of us children huddled, instinctively, in the opposite corner from our aunt, while I was fortunate to have Uncle Archibald to my immediate left, with Mother and Father next to him.

For some time none of us spoke. We could hear the rain coming down, and the hum of the wind, but it sounded very distant. I felt scared but less so than when I had been outside. In my heart I believed that the pantry protected us, since it was so small I assumed that no storm would have the patience to probe for its precise location. Frederick broke the silence. "Father," he asked, "what if we need to . . ." and he glanced down at his dark blue knickers, which were uncharacteristically clean.

"There's a chamber pot," Father pointed at the long shelf several feet above his head that ran the length of the small room, on which Mother and I had placed our china, which sat wrapped in bath towels and dish rags. "If need be we shall draw a blanket—"

Aunt Grace interrupted him by exclaiming briefly, only keeping her taut mouth closed so that the wail seemed to come from behind her head. She and Uncle Edwin had brought in a picnic basket they must have packed the day before, which he opened, removing a dishcloth over which he carefully dribbled a smattering of water from the large pitcher to his right before dabbing at her forehead while she fanned herself with her hand.

With Aunt Grace clearly on the verge of delirium, we all knew to be quiet and sat there glumly, listening to the storm. For several minutes even Uncle Archibald was still, and in my mind I wondered who would begin to fidget first, he or my brother Frederick. It ended up being my uncle. I had forgotten to take note of his barometer, which he had placed against the wall on his left side, in between him and my mother, but after what must have seemed to him to be an excruciatingly long time, he stood up and, crouching sharply—since the pantry was located under the stairwell of our home and our end of the room was beneath the lowest part of the stairs—pulled the barometer out so that it loomed in front of him. Then he sat back down, but not before withdrawing a handkerchief from his back pocket, which he used to wipe down the glass. He slowly rocked the barometer very gently on its iron base so that it inched toward him. Then he leaned forward, withdrawing his monocle from his vest pocket, and stared intently at the mercury level in the glass.

"Yes, still falling, still falling," he said softly. Jerry and Jack leaned across my lap, trying to get a better look, but I scooted forward to preserve my vantage point. I could see the line of yellow liquid in the tube perfectly, and could even count the marks between the numbers etched on the side of the glass. It was, I felt, somehow right that at long last I could enjoy studying this mysterious instrument of measurement up close, and I thrilled at the thought that perhaps Uncle Archibald had subtly arranged our single-file entrance into the pantry so that I would be seated next to him.

"Yes, well below twenty-eight, well below." His whiskers trembled as he exhaled. "This shall be a truly ferocious storm. Absolutely ferocious."

Uncle Archibald's breath condensed on the glass and, as if summoned by his assessment, the storm did seem suddenly to pick up strength. We could hear the raindrops pounding against the roof and the boarded-up windows, their tone deeper and more serious than when—during other storms—they merely plucked against thin glass, and above and beneath this noise rose the sound of the wind, which had begun to scream and hiss. I nestled close to my uncle, who—a few minutes later—conducted another reading, at which point my father, the recipient of a withering stare from Aunt Grace and a look of absolute horror from my mother, asked his brother to desist from such outbursts. Uncle Archibald nodded glumly and gently rocked the barometer back against the wall. Not content that it sit there so brazenly, however, my father took off his jacket and draped it over the iron stand, hiding the instrument from our view.

We all sat still for what seemed like years, listening to the storm, which continued to rage but did not seem to be increasing in strength. I had noticed Uncle Edwin some time before, looking uncomfortable, and first I attributed it to the storm before realizing, as he gently opened the lid of his picnic basket, that of course he was hungry. He withdrew a tin, wrapped in a piece of newspaper, that he opened, withdrawing a piece of stone crab that had already been removed from its shell. He placed the piece in his mouth before holding out the tin in our direction. "Please," he mumbled, making a point of looking at me, since he knew I would be the least likely to accept his offer, as eating shellfish produced a red rash on my neck. My brothers declined as well, and Uncle Edwin licked his fingers before eating another claw.

"Odd, that we are to remain ignorant of a means of measuring the storm's power," Uncle Archibald spoke in a rush, his voice higher than his brothers' and far more fluttery, "whilst we indulge in food that can do nothing save make our dwelling place smell like Morgan Bartlum's bait shop."

Uncle Edwin snickered in response, permitting himself one more piece before putting the tin back in the picnic basket. I confess to having smelled nothing disagreeable at all, just the wax from the candles, Uncle Archibald's worn suit, and a hint of rum that always hung about him faintly, like a halo. We sat in silence for the next hour or so, save for Aunt Grace, from whose mouth an exasperated sigh would occasionally escape. Along with Archibald, I had expected Frederick to put up resistance to such close quarters, but instead he fell asleep shortly after Edwin's next sampling of stone crab. When he awoke a short time later, it was because he needed to empty his bladder, which required my father to pull the chamber pot down from the shelf and then look around the room with dread. "I do think, Jeremiah," Uncle Archibald said coolly, "that it would not be unsafe for young Frederick to relieve himself on the other side of the door." Father agreed, and after Frederick was done Jack and Jerry soon followed his example.

As the hours passed, my brothers nodded off while the storm pounded our home, occasionally causing the frame to shift but otherwise carrying on less obtrusively than I would have thought. I was no longer frightened so much as bored. I could not sleep and wanted to fetch my book, which was just a few feet away in the living room, but to have asked permission, I knew, would have riled my father, so I kept silent and passed the time sneaking glances at my older relatives. Mother stared blankly at the floor for one hour, and then another, her expression remaining unchanged, only her nostrils thinning whenever she inhaled. Father shifted uncomfortably again and again, his fingers drumming his fore-arm impatiently, the heel of his leather shoe occasionally tapping the tile beneath us. I could not determine whether or not Aunt Grace slept, as her bonnet was pulled tight around her face, but I suspected that she did, since she displayed no reaction to Uncle Edwin's systematic emptying of the contents of the picnic basket into his mouth: first the remaining bits of stone crab, then sugar cookies, a banana, half a loaf of Cuban bread, and finally a healthy slab of cured beef. Although Uncle Archibald was largely silent, he did pass me several pieces of taffy, and apologized more than once for his right hand, which had begun, after several hours, to quiver slightly, and then finally shake more or less constantly, knocking into the sleeve of my dress over and over again.

A tremendous crash roused all of us. It seemed to have come from the front of the house and presented Uncle Archibald the opportunity to check his timepiece. He showed me its face and barely managed a thin smile. It was eight o'clock in the evening. We had been sequestered together for more than seven hours, and the night had barely begun. Perhaps sensing this, or feel-ing—I think now, with the benefit of hindsight—desperate for a drink but afraid to produce his flask in front of us, lest my father admonish him, Uncle Archibald stood up abruptly, knocking his head against the low ceiling.

"I daresay," he rubbed his crown furiously, the thin strands of his hair standing on end, "I must excuse myself, tempest be damned!" And he placed his straw hat on his head, unlatched the door, and walked out of the pantry. We all waited breathlessly for his return. The minutes went by, more than seemed appropriate. I thought of him never returning; of course I did not think of him dead, I did not understand yet what death was, but I thought of his barometer sitting there in the pantry where he had left it, gathering dust, its powers dissipated since no one else could interpret its signs.

The door opened abruptly and again we all started. Without

saying anything, Uncle Archibald walked over to his instrument and pulled it into the center of the pantry. Then he held his monocle up again to his left eye and reexamined the glass tube. "We have," he announced, "passed through the greatest threat posed by this storm. The winds, from my observation, are not hurricane force, and barometric pressure has begun to rise. Indeed, I see no reason for us to remain in these narrow confines. You have, Jeremiah, lost the large banyan tree in front, and a good many branches and leaves, but the exterior of the house appears to have made it through quite well."

We sat still, and looked over at Father for permission to move. He rose slowly to his feet, on the one hand surely loath to trust his brother on the subject of the storm, but on the other hand as desperate as all of us to move out of the pantry, the walls of which seemed to be tightening by the minute. Uncle Edwin assured our release by lumbering to his feet and then uncharacteristically yanking his wife to hers.

"So that is all you have to say for your mighty hurricane, Archie? One tree!" he bellowed.

"It was a bad one," Uncle Archibald smoothed down his whiskers. He seemed not the least bit rattled by the fact that his youngest brother was addressing him directly for the first time in six years. "Perhaps not here, but wherever the eye passed was very bad. It was a concentrated demon, yes, but a demon nonetheless."

Edwin waved his hand at him, then picked up his picnic basket and walked by him gruffly, out into the dining room. "You give voice to delusions," he grumbled as he passed through the doorway. "You always have."

Aunt Grace nodded her head in agreement as she followed behind him. "Delusions!" she snickered, unfastening her bonnet, presumably because we were no longer threatened by the weather.

Their dramatic exit was diminished by the fact that, even if we were not in the eye of the hurricane, we were in the midst of a significant storm, which meant that our father could not drive them home. So Aunt Grace and Uncle Edwin marched out of the pantry and, after a brief pause, into our dark living room. While Father surveyed the outside with Uncle Archibald and Jerry,

Mother and I brought out some pork from the icebox and made the best sandwiches we could.

The rest of the evening I can barely recall: just a quick meal, with the sound of branches breaking outside and the rain pattering madly, and a sense of relief when Father sent us off to bed. Frederick asked permission to sleep with me, since he didn't want to be alone, and we hugged each other under the sheets as the storm raged on. Before drifting into sleep more easily than I would have ever imagined, I remember making a deal with the God in which I only vaguely believed: if he permitted us safe passage through the storm, I would no longer bemoan the tiny island on which I lived, a place where nothing seemed to happen save the occasional tropical and great depression.

The next morning, work around our home began early. Father helped the boys take down the boards from the windows, saw the banyan tree into removable pieces, and mend our fence, several slats of which had been broken by the tree. According to my brothers, Uncle Edwin watched them work from alongside the house, until he spied Curtis Anderson passing by in his truck. Uncle Edwin waved him down in the hopes that he might be driving over to the Atlantic side of the island, where his mother, Mrs. Anderson, the town librarian, lived, and indeed he was. Mr. Anderson offered Uncle Edwin and Aunt Grace a ride home and they were gone in a flash, bidding us all goodbye with hurried, stiff waves. By that time, Mother and I had finished restoring our china to the kitchen, and I was given permission to remain on the front steps of our porch. That was where I was perched when a boy rode up on a bicycle and asked for my father. He was from the East Coast Railway Office downtown, he explained, handing him an envelope before tipping his blue hat and biking off hurriedly. The phone lines were down, so it was impossible to place any calls, but nonetheless, the delivery of a letter seemed serious, even ominous, and Jerry and Jack set down their saws in order to watch our father's reaction. He read the correspondence slowly, and when he placed the letter back in the envelope I knew something was wrong because he called out his brother's name in an urgent, nearly hysterical way. "Archie! Archie!" he cried. And Frederick, who had been piling branches on the sidewalk, stopped in his tracks.

It turned out the eye of the hurricane had passed over Upper Matecumbe Key, striking the train that had been sent down to rescue the highway workers. It was overturned, that was all the letter said about the train, and that forty miles of track between Marathon and Tavernier had been wiped out. There would be no train service from Miami for some time, we didn't know for how long.

"We must," Father was pacing in front of the house, the corduroy pants he wore when he worked outside streaked with dirt and brown stains from the fallen leaves, "we must fetch our assets. Today, before they are picked over."

Uncle Archibald had rushed over when my father called for him, and his suspenders still hung around his waist. He was wearing one of his old Cuban shirts, the collar of which brimmed with shaving cream. He shook his head in disagreement. "I'm not sure I'll be able to get the *Edith Kermit* running; it might have been damaged in the storm."

"You must get it running. We have no choice, Archie, otherwise we're ruined."·

"Even if we can make it up the Keys, Jeremiah, I doubt the linens will have come through the storm very well."

"It's all we have. In the current situation . . ." He shook his head. The matter was grave enough that he couldn't be bothered to shield us from the discussion. "No, we must recoup our goods. There is nothing else we can do." He looked around the yard furtively, as if he might find a solution to our problem in the shrubs and hedges that seemed to have made it through the storm quite well. Then he addressed us directly. "Children, we are making a trip up the Keys today, to Islamorada—"

"Jeremiah!" I had not noticed the appearance of my mother in the doorway, or heard her raise her voice above a whisper in many months, and the shock of her booming voice made me rise to my feet. "Jeremiah, I do not want the children going up the Keys, not after a storm. Can't you and Edwin round up some workers from the store?"

"My dear Martha, if we cannot salvage our goods, we will have no way of paying the workers for the day's labor. We must go together, all of us, save Edwin and Grace, whose constitutions would not bear such a day. We will need as many hands as possible."

"A young woman, retrieving sheets . . ." Mother beckoned toward me and I burned suddenly with fear at the thought of being left at home. I had been north of Marathon Key only a few times before, and in Miami just once, so any trip was to be treasured, regardless of the circumstances. Plus, the thought of hearing of the adventure secondhand from my brothers, none of whom could tell a tale straight from beginning to end, meant that I would never know what exactly had transpired. I began to plot how I might somehow hide myself aboard the *Edith Kermit*, only that ended up being unnecessary.

"You and Mary may remain in the boat, Martha," my father said by way of reply. "I'm afraid we will need you both in order to fold the sheets. Besides, I cannot leave you here alone, and I will need Archie's help with the boat." He paused. "It will be good for the children to see what supports our family, Martha. We have far more than most."

Mother said nothing; she just motioned to me so that I would follow her inside, which I gladly did, excited by the prospect that our work in the kitchen would be in the service of a voyage to Upper Matecumbe Key. We put what little food we had remaining in our own picnic basket, and filled two pitchers of water from the overflowing cistern in back. Then I was permitted to put on my recreational clothes: a coarse cloth dress that fit easily over my swimming suit, which Mother suggested I wear in case I got wet, and a light shawl. She elected not to change out of her black satin dress, although she added a plain, yellow bonnet that seemed, in my view, not quite to match.

By this time the boys were also ready for the voyage, having put on their swimming trunks, plus long-sleeved, linen shirts to minimize mosquito bites. Our car, a Model A sedan, would have never been able to pass through the streets, filled as they were with rainwater and broken branches, so we walked to the *Edith Kermit*, which was only a block away, anchored on the near side of Garrison Bight. Uncle Archibald met us there, having walked directly over to see if he could get his boat running. None of the vessels in the bight appeared to have been damaged, although a few had been loosed from their moorings and were floating in the middle of the inlet, while the palm trees that lined the water along what would become Roosevelt Boulevard had been stripped of their coconuts and canopies. We loaded the craft, placing the picnic basket and pitchers of water in the small aft cabin, and the various tools gathered by the boys in the metal container in the bow, previously half filled with a few life preservers and fishing tackle, while Uncle Archibald cursed and coaxed the diesel engine to life. When it finally turned over, spewing black and then finally gray smoke into the air, he was able to verify that we had enough fuel for the trip up to Islamorada, but not enough to return.

"And there will be no petroleum available in all of the Keys that lie before us?" my father asked him. Uncle Archibald shrugged. "I cannot predict the situation that we will encounter," was his simple reply. He still believed that the atmospheric dip recorded by his barometer had exacted a terrible blow somewhere in our world, although none of us did. Not even I, his most faithful follower, was willing to dismiss what I saw around me: the expected aftereffects of a serious storm, but nothing more.

Uncle Archibald let Frederick unloop the ropes that kept the *Edith Kermit* tied to the dock and soon we had passed out of the bight and through Cow Key Channel. The water was like glass and once we had passed the reef and were in the Atlantic Uncle Archibald opened up the engine. Jerry, Jack, Frederick, and I quickly moved to the bow and tasted the froth of the salt foam on our lips as we skimmed over waves and skirted the coral fingers surrounding Pelican Shoal.

How long the trip took I cannot recall, as I have never in my long life had reason to do it again. At least several hours, long enough for the light to change markedly. Although we made good time for most of the voyage, when it came time to turn toward Islamorada, Uncle Archibald became confused by his map. Upper Matecumbe did not seem to line up where it was supposed to, at least not at first. Our boat slowed to a crawl, taking the current as it circled around the key right in the bow, so that the waves and splashes sent us scurrying into the stern, where Mother sat alone on the back bench of the boat, her hands gripping her forearms, her feet pressed up against a coil of rope.

In fact, Uncle Archibald had not misread his map; the banks of Upper Matecumbe were just unrecognizable, having been shorn of all foliage and stripped of the few wooden shacks and homes that had sat undisturbed for years. Boats were now all around us, many with men at their sides, pulling and tugging large pieces of driftwood aboard. We slowed even more, the *Edith Kermit* now bobbing up and down as much as moving forward, so that the mosquitoes began to flicker around our faces.

It was right then, or at least in my mind's recollection, as I swatted at an insect, that the images around me slowed and crystallized. We were now within shouting distance of the first vessel and I saw that it was not driftwood these men were pulling and yanking at but bodies, the limbs yellow and stiffened, their clothing torn and drooping on their frames. And then I saw, in the water on our right, the bloated face of a young girl, the eyes glazed open, her neck swollen and black, her naked body translucent under the water, and heard my mother scream and felt myself grabbed and pushed into the aft cabin by Uncle Archibald. Father brought Mother and Frederick down after me, ordering the three of us to stay seated, only Mother had not stopped screaming, and now Frederick was crying and pressing his hands to his ears. The smell of rum, once stashed beneath the bench on which we sat, was thick in the stale air and I remember not quite being able to catch my breath and shaking my head, trying to shed the image I had of the dead girl in the water, the face that would haunt my dreams for years and years to come.

So I ended up being there, in the aftermath of the Labor Day Hurricane, but only somewhat. Yes, I was in the boat with my brothers, but I didn't see all that they did, and they never told me what I missed, not that I asked. We spoke of that day only with our eyes, never our mouths. I do recall clearly what transpired next. A vessel approached ours, cutting through the water cleanly, and after its engine cut off a voice identified itself loudly as that of a Coast Guard captain.

"We are directing the relief boats to the other side," he yelled out.

"We have not come to offer relief," my father shouted back. "We have come to reclaim our linens and towels from the derailed cars of the East Coast Railway."

"Sir, those cars are filled with the dead," came the reply. "You have brought your boat into hell, my dear man. You are in hell."

My mother exclaimed once more, before wailing in a high-pitched moan, and then fell silent. I had placed my arms around Frederick and squeezed him tight.

"I speak of goods which we own and lease to the Railway . . ." My father was not himself either. He had always thought he could control the world around him, and we were all witnessing that day proof to the contrary.

"Do you hear me, sir?" the captain continued. "We have dozens of dead on this key. There are bodies everywhere: in the surf, in the few trees that survived the winds, and in your precious railway cars. If you cannot help us assist the suffering then you must leave. Forget your goods, sir, and thank God for your life."

The engine of the cutter kicked in and the boat sped away, its wake rocking our vessel. Now there were other noises, other engines, shouts, even cries. We were closer to shore and I heard Jack, of all people, my levelheaded and unflappable brother, exclaim, "Papa, no! Please, Papa!" And then there was Uncle Archibald, cursing like a man possessed, and our boat suddenly turning sharply to the left side (is that port?), picking up speed, and then several minutes of silence as the engine hummed, before the door opened and Father—his hair disheveled, his shirt untucked— asked me to hold my mother's arms while he meted out an inordinate dose of her Dover's powder, which I did not know was an opiate until years and years later, when I saw it described as such in a Victorian medical book I thought to purchase at a yard sale because I liked its binding. And then no noises for a while, except the diesel engine, or at least none that I remember.

We made it back only so far as Lower Matecumbe, staying close to land so that we could make it ashore as soon as we ran out of fuel. When the engine cut out we sat, the three of us, in the aft cabin, Frederick's whimpers now audible with the engine noise subsided, my mother, the powder dissolved fully in her bloodstream, looking out at nothing, her mouth pinched in a ghostly half smile. Uncle Archibald and the boys had to call to the shore for several minutes before a rowboat could be scrounged up. Then my father descended again. "You must go ashore here, Mary," he said to me. "Jerry will go with you and Frederick, then Jack and Mother. You must all take the ferry to No Name Key. Archibald and I shall stay with the boat."

I struggled to my feet, the weight of my young brother heavy on my chest. I thought of the dead girl in the water: her fair hair fanning out, the eyes so savage and dumb.

"Do not look about you," my father said, steadying me with his hand. His face was drained of its color and he looked very old. "This is where the camps were for the highway workers so it might be very bad. Promise me you shall not look about."

I nodded. Frederick was pried from me, screaming, while I stepped down into the rowboat before a young man, his eyes blazing, who sat at the oars. He wore overalls with nothing underneath them and his arms were thin as wires. They handed Frederick back to me and, together with Jack, we were rowed ashore.

The mind adapts to anything; it is quite astounding. From the brief time we left the *Edith Kermit* to our disembarkment on Lower Matecumbe, for the space of maybe one hundred yards, the mind adjusted to the sight of the floating dead, the dismembered dead, the decapitated dead, and then, once we were ashore, the half-buried dead, the naked dead, covered with blowflies (their hums filling the dark air), the dead with their faces somehow melted off, the dead that looked almost as if they were living. Farther up the beach, some the bodies had been placed in wooden coffins, while others were piled together and wrapped in sheets, their feet pointing up in the air. In a tight circle, the three of us waited for Mother and Jerry, then joined the crowd at the dock and boarded the last ferry of the day: a boat filled with refugees from the storm we had missed, but not entirely.

At No Name Key, Jerry recognized a classmate whose boat could hold three more for Key West; otherwise, Frederick, Mother, and I would have had to wait on the docks with the others who had no one to pick them up. We traveled home slowly. The seas were choppy and our vessel was small and overloaded. Jerry and Jack did not return until late the next day, and Uncle Archibald and Father two days after that. Stubble and grime had overtaken Uncle Archibald's fine moustache, which would disappear for good when he shaved the next day, while my father's own face was sunburned and cracked. He carried, in the crook of his arm, a handful of badly soiled sheets, and while we all wondered what they had encountered when they had finally made it to the train, none of us asked; the small bundle of worthless goods said enough.

The Florida East Coast Railway declared bankruptcy a few days later, and Columbia Laundry Service closed its doors at the end of that month. As a favor, father was given a job at the Casa Marina Hotel, but he was inappropriately dispositioned for the hospitality industry, which had ground to a halt anyway, and he quit before he could be relieved of his post. Satisfactory employment would elude him for more than a decade but he never stopped working and managed, somehow, to feed us. It helped that Jerry and then Jack got work with the Florida State Highway Department, and were on the crew that finished the Overseas Highway, although Jack would have his fibula shattered by an iron support beam on Big Pine Key and would never walk without pain again.

They never restored train service to Key West. With our business closed, Aunt Grace and Uncle Edwin moved up to Saint Augustine, where her family was from. It was to be a temporary arrangement, but like most residents who moved away at that time, they never returned to the island. A year later, desperate for money, we were forced to sell Uncle Archibald's house and dispose of his bicycle parts and tires and metal frames. He moved in with us, into the back room behind the kitchen, but he could not stand being in our home with nothing to do. There seemed, in the face of such punishing bleakness, little reason to think of fantastic contrivances such as water bikes, and by the time I was twenty Uncle Archibald spent his days and nights on Caroline Street with the other town drunks. The lilt in his speech, the dart in his eye, and the beautiful flowers in his lapel were by then just a memory. Until he died, many years later, I could not reclaim his image as my dapper uncle; in fact, I hated him for the way he smelled of rainwater and fried plantains and for how he tripped over his consonants.

My mother was institutionalized in 1939. We saw her each Christmas for five years following but by 1944 the opium had drained her memory entirely, turning her skin the color and texture of flour, and we stopped visiting. She died a year later, as did Frederick on Okinawa, fighting the Japanese.

I'll tell you what I think and you may take it or leave it as you wish. I think that most families are very fragile. Those impressive genealogies we have all seen, say in the inside covers of books, give false hope. Most families are like the torchwood and palms that somehow grow on hard coral and limestone, and then one day encounter unanticipated wind and rain and are wiped clean away. And that we who somehow survive remember so little, and pass on even less, is a merciful and melancholic thing—more merciful than melancholic, but only just.

Central Square

I met Andrea during one of those miserable February days in Boston when it rains and snows at the same time. I was on my lunch break and just because I was bored I took the T over to Copley Place from Commonwealth Ave, where I worked at a futon store facing B.U. I wandered through the covered bridge they've got there, the one that connects the mall to the hotel, and looked at the different carts they had, all of them selling artisan stuff—clay bowls and tiny wooden boxes and bookends and ceramic mugs and picture frames made out of tin foil and candlestick holders shaped like giraffes and those little Russian toy dolls that all fit into each other. I checked out one cart after the other, went by all the vendors sitting on their stools, reading newspapers or playing solitaire, and just about at the end of the bridge there was a cart filled with Latin American crafts, rugs and ponchos and these brightly colored knit caps, so for no reason I tried one on and looked at myself in this little mirror they had and then I glanced over at the woman sitting there. She was youngish, at first I put her right at eighteen, and it wasn't like she was beautiful, it really wasn't, although she did have these green eyes that were about ready to jump out of their sockets. Her hair was all brown and frizzy, but her skin was real smooth and tight and I remember thinking that was nice because good skin—not just clear skin but good skin—is real rare.

So I smiled and asked her how I looked and she said, *Very good*, with a thick accent, so I asked her if she was just saying that so I'd buy the cap and she said, *Sorry?* and I said it slower and she said, *No!* and I said, *In that case, I'll take it.* She told me it was eight bucks and I gave her the money and asked where she was from and she said Chile and I asked her where that was and she said, *No one knows where Chile is!* I told her not to take me as an example of what people knew because I didn't know shit, but I didn't say *shit*, I said something like *a darn thing* and smiled again. When I asked if she wanted to get a drink that night, she said, *Drink?* but sort of suspiciously so I said, *Coffee?* and she smiled and said, *Coffee, yes, coffee!* I told her I'd come back around five and she said, *Sorry?* again so I repeated myself. Then I walked off and spent the rest of my break poking around the other end of the mall, staying inside—because the snow was really coming down by that time—and I got sort of restless because there weren't many stores at that end of the mall but going to the other end would have meant either walking outside or past her cart again and I didn't want to do either. So I ended up trying jeans on at the Gap but their jeans never fit me right and then I went back to work and Jeff, my boss, barked at me because I had been gone for so long but I didn't care because at least I had something to do that night and Jeff didn't scare me one bit—he acted like the futon store was all his idea but his dad had put up the money, everyone knew that.

That night, we had coffee on the other side of the mall. She ordered a skinny short double latte with extra foam, barely pausing between the words, and I tried to get some black coffee but the woman behind the counter asked if I wanted the house blend or the light roast or the special and I got rattled and ordered one of the tiny coffees instead. She asked me if I meant espresso and I nodded my head. Once we were sitting down I said to her that I bet she got a free cup of coffee every night because she was so cute and she blushed and said, *No!* and her eyes were just beaming and I thought she was just as sweet as a girl could be and it wasn't even like I was thinking of trying to get her clothes off, nothing at all like that, she just looked at me so sweetly I couldn't disappear right after the coffee. So I asked her if she wanted to see a movie sometime and she said *Yes, very much,* and we walked by the cinema afterward and there was a Spanish movie playing there, a real popular movie too (I don't remember the title), and I would have never noticed it but she did right away. I was thinking that seeing a movie with subtitles sounded like a drag because you don't go to a movie to read, but I said that was fine so we made plans to see it the next day after she closed up the cart and I said goodbye to her. She said goodbye and we sort of waved at each other from about four feet away and I headed off in the opposite direction she was going in—which was actually toward the T but I didn't want to walk behind her or anything—and about a half second later I called out to her, *Hey! What's your name, anyway?* because I had completely forgotten to ask her, and I had to chase after her and tug her on the arm to get her attention because she didn't so much as glance back when I called out to her. She laughed without making a sound when I made a crack about us forgetting some of the basics—she had, like, a silent laugh—and that's when she told me her name, Andrea, and it didn't sound like the sort of name I thought she'd have. When I told her my name she stood there and said it out loud like she was rehearsing it—*Peter, Peter.* She said it while I waved goodbye.

I hated the movie; the main woman in it cooked all the time because she was in love with this guy and it made me hungry at first but then it annoyed me because she just couldn't say what was on her mind. I thought about putting my arm around Andrea, or touching her leg, but I didn't. She was dressed just nice enough to make me feel like maybe I should have worn my good leather shoes with my jeans instead of my Bean boots and I probably would have worn nicer shoes if the slush and everything outside hadn't been so bad. Besides, it was just a movie, so I hadn't given it much thought.

I asked her if she wanted to go have a drink afterward and she said *Drink!* and I said it didn't have to be a *drink drink* (I swear people who overheard us sometimes must have thought we were retarded). She said *Sorry?* so I went on about how maybe we could go somewhere else, outside of the mall, and she said, *No!* real seriously, shaking her head and looking down at her watch. About then I was beginning to wonder what in the hell I had gotten myself into, and I looked down to think about what to do and saw her black heels again and decided she was probably wearing the nicest outfit she had, and I was in my Bean boots—bad move. So I sort of shrugged my shoulders and said, *Coffee?* and she nodded her head and smiled real big.

I had another espresso. She had the same latte thing, said it was her favorite. I was sort of peeved about sitting in the coffee shop, for no real reason other than it wasn't what I had pictured us doing, but it was hard staying mad because she tried to cheer me up by talking a lot. She must have been nervous because she started saying stuff I didn't understand. Just watching her try so hard made me feel good. She asked me about my family and I told her how my dad had died the year before—prostate cancer—and she took hold of my hand when I told her that and I started talking about it, about how we had never gotten along on account of his vicious temper, which always flared up after he had been drinking, which meant every night around six. The only thing the two of us could really talk about was my mother because we both just loved her so much, and I explained that my mom still lived in Lowell in the house where I had grown up and that I had quit my job as a bartender and moved to Boston the year before in the hopes of getting a real job. I wanted to work in advertising because I figured—since I had always watched a lot of television and kind of kept track of the commercials that had worked on me—I'd be good at it, but since I hadn't gone to college I couldn't get an interview anywhere, so I ended up working in this futon store on Beacon Street, at first just to make a little bit of dough while I sent out résumés, but when nothing came of my job hunt I decided that even though the pay, with commissions, was shit,

I'd just be content with it for a while because it was easy work and I was good at it.

I didn't tell her the other reason, maybe the real reason, I had moved to Boston in the first place. On account of bartending and my friends and everything I was drinking way too much my last year in Lowell, had even pushed my mom around one night when I was hammered, which had scared me some. Everything else, though, I told Andrea, sort of in a rush, and I didn't even assume she could follow all of it but she seemed to be listening and then I caught her glancing at her watch and so finally I asked her if she needed to go and she said, *Yes*, nodding her head, eyes so big then, just fixed on me—thought maybe she might cry and I asked myself if I wanted her to because it's usually a good sign if they cry but that was the last thing I wanted from her, that I knew. We left the shop and said goodbye at our little spot, right before the escalators, and after I said goodbye I started walking the other way and then decided to double back and follow her up the escalator and I saw her in the crowd, which was thick, and she headed toward the south entrance. There was a little old guy all bundled up in one of those lumpy red parkas you can get at Salvation Army, and he was waiting there and I ducked into the Body Shop and picked up one of the loofahs while I watched. He pointed at his watch and Andrea nodded her head and he shook his hands at her and she just nodded her head and then they left.

Instead of taking the T straight home to Jamaica Plain, where I lived at the time, I started stopping by her cart every day after work. We'd have coffee. It was weird. I never said I was coming by again; I never was real sure myself if I would, but I kept on doing it. And it was real clear, right off the bat, somehow it was understood that we weren't going to set foot out of that goddamn mall together. I don't quite know how she laid that law down but I don't know how we communicated all that we did. Lots of times I don't think she understood what I was saying—her eyes would get real big, or she'd look away—and sometimes I couldn't follow her and I'd just nod my head and say yes. Most of the time she'd just smile and sometimes take my hand, although not always, and lots of times she'd do her silent laugh and I loved that. The more time we spent together the younger I thought she looked until, after a week or two, I decided I wasn't going to ask how old she was. Besides, even if I had asked, that wouldn't have meant anything, her age; she was young, regardless. When I got around to asking her what her father did she just said, *laborer,* and when I asked her what her mother did she put her thumbs in the air and wiggled them and it took a good five minutes before I understood that she knitted and made all of that stuff that was on the cart. She said she had three kid brothers and one older brother who was working on the Big Dig and was very strong and used a jackhammer and the sentence sounded kind of rehearsed and I wondered if her dad told her to say that to me, just to give me something to think about.

After a while I was drinking triple shots of espresso. It didn't seem any healthier than drinking scotch or bourbon, the way the caffeine made my heart race, but I didn't forget stuff either. We'd walk around the mall, looking in the store windows, people-watching. Every night at five to seven she'd say that she had to go and I figured that her father was waiting for her down at the south entrance, although I didn't ever follow her again to see.

She talked a lot about being Catholic. She asked me early on if I was Catholic and I said that was how I was brought up but that I hadn't gone to church in a real long time and that seemed to concern her and when I'd see her early in the week she'd ask if I'd been to church and when I'd say no she'd always get quiet for a moment. Finally I told her to stop asking me about stuff like that because she reminded me of my mom and it made me feel guilty, not so much that I wasn't going to church but that I wasn't calling my mom more often than I was, or going home to Lowell to see her. Since leaving I kind of didn't want to go back, maybe on account of my friends partying so much, or just because of the thought of being back in the house, which had seemed real empty since Dad had died. Even though he had been a jerk most of the time, it still didn't feel right for him not to be sitting on the couch in the living room, or out on the back porch, listening to the Red Sox on the radio.

The one time I lost it early on, when I just felt like a lab rat, pacing around that goddamn mall all the time, was when I kicked over the garbage can in front of the luggage store on the first level and stormed off. I was going to walk home and never come back. I was going to get my life in order—find a real job, start making good money, move to the Back Bay—but I couldn't walk more than a block; I just couldn't leave her, why I don't know. So I went back into the mall and walked through the atrium on the first floor and found her sitting on the edge of the fountain there with her eyes closed, and I said to her, *What are you doing here? What are you looking at?* and she said, *I'm praying for you,* and I didn't say anything.

Once I remember she was using the bathroom and I wandered out in front of the Brookstone store and they had a knife in the window that I thought looked sort of cool and when she came out she asked me what I was looking at and I said, *That knife there.* It was real sturdy looking, about a four-inch blade, stainless steel, black metal casing. We looked at it together and then walked away and I didn't think anything of it at the time.

I don't know how to put it, the way I felt for her. It was sort of feverish. Sometimes I'd go into Copley on my lunch break and just hover right around the bridge and watch her sit there on her stool, reading. She read these detective books written in Spanish (I thought it was funny, I don't know why). Anyway, I wouldn't even go talk to her, unless she saw me, then I'd walk over and ask her if I could bring her lunch because she couldn't leave her cart. A lot of times in the early afternoon her mom'd be there—putting new stuff out—so I wouldn't hang around.

For the next several weeks, until the middle of April or so, I'd go by after work and we'd have coffee and walk around the mall. After a time I just started to lose it. I was taking two-hour lunch breaks and spending my nights, from seven o'clock on, sort of hanging out in my apartment by myself, thinking of Andrea, and I started to drink again. I hadn't realized I had stopped drinking completely until I started up again, and at first it was okay but pretty soon I was drinking like I had back in Lowell. Then, the next thing I knew, I was on this Old Crow kick and I was boozing pretty hard every night. I began to take a flask with me to work and when I was with Andrea sometimes I'd sneak a shot or two in the bathroom. She never seemed to notice when I drank; it was like she didn't know that alcohol had even been invented, which made me wonder what her family did at night. There was that time, right around Patriot's Day, when I kicked that garbage can and after that I didn't come by for almost a week and in the meantime I got the talk from Jeff about caring, giving it my all, the whole load of shit, and I decided I wasn't going to go by that mall anymore. That same night I went by and she was sitting there and looked real sad—eyes shrunk up in their sockets—and when she saw me she started to cry and I said, *No!* I said, *Don't ever cry over me!* and she said, *Sorry,* but without raising the last bit of the word into a question. We went out for coffee and I went to the bathroom and finished my flask and when I came back to the table she took out a little package and gave it to me and it was the knife we had looked at and I said I couldn't take it but she just smiled so I opened it up and looked at it. It was a nice knife, the hinge was real tight and the blade wasn't big but it just gleamed, it was so clean, and I said, *Thank you, Andrea. You shouldn't have bought this for me. I'll take it, but you really shouldn't have bought it for me.* I put it in my pocket and she blushed and I made her promise she wouldn't buy me anything else and she said she wouldn't and we left the coffee shop and at the foot of the escalators I hugged her and she hugged me back and I kissed her on the cheek and then I turned and kissed her very gently on the lips and I felt her body up against mine and she kissed me without opening her mouth and I kissed her and held her and pressed her against me and kissed her and she kissed me and then she opened her mouth and I pressed her harder against me and we kissed like this for several minutes until she said that she had to go. It was almost seven-thirty.

The next night I went by her cart and I was already a little tipsy and we went and had coffee and walked around and went to the fountain where she had sat once and prayed for me. We began to kiss and she leaned back on one arm and I leaned forward and we slowly reclined on the side of the fountain and I kissed her very hard and she kissed me back and I lay down on top of her for just a moment and then a security guard came by and said that this was a public place and Andrea was real embarrassed and I said to him, *We know where we are!* only louder than I meant to say it. He walked off and Andrea looked at me funny and it was ruined. We walked around for a while and she held my hand because she knew how angry I was and when we got to the escalators her dad was standing there, wearing that red parka of his, and she spoke to him loudly in Spanish, and he spoke to her, looking at me, and she said, *Peter, this is my father,* and I held my hand out and he said, *Howoldareyou?* so that I could barely understand him. He seemed to smell the bourbon on me, at least he acted like he smelled something, but I was probably just being paranoid. Andrea spoke to him in Spanish and I just smiled and said it was nice to meet him and finally he took my hand and shook it and Andrea said goodnight and they walked off. Right in front of the luggage store she turned her head to look at me and I waved.

The next day, after work, I stopped by a liquor store on the way over to the mall and bought a fifth of bourbon and drank a good bit of it before I got to her cart. When she saw me she was quick to say she was sorry about her dad standing by the escalators the night before and I said, *No big deal.* I felt real mellow about the whole thing—work had gone well, I had sold something like eight futons and I had a nice buzz—and when she closed up the cart she started walking toward the coffee shop like she always did but I said, *Where are you going?* She said, *For coffee, no?* and just because I was so buzzed maybe, just for that alone, I said, *Coffee's fine, but this mall, I've had it with this mall,* and she said, *Coffee?* and I said, *Andrea, I don't want to have coffee in this mall* and she said, *I am sorry, Peter, I am sorry,* and I said, *Are you not allowed to go out of this mall with me? Is that what you're telling me?* And she said, *Not allowed?* And I said, *Jesus Fuck!* much louder than I meant to and when I said it she was a few feet away from me but she rushed toward me and put her arms up around my neck and said, *Peter, Peter, Peter,* and I wasn't talking to her now, it wasn't directed toward her, but I said, *Get the fuck away from me!* and just like that I wasn't mellow anymore. She grabbed me real hard and I needed to get away from her and outside of that place because it was closing in on me. I said, *Let go! Let go!* and she was sobbing, going, *Peter! Peter!* and finally I took a hold of her shoulders and pushed her off of me but I was so fired up and everything that I pushed her harder than I meant to and she went into the cart real awkwardly so that her shoulder hit against it and made an awful sound—like wood snapping—and she fell over and cried out real loud in Spanish, not a word so much as a yell but it was definitely in Spanish. The next thing I knew all the fucking vendors ran over, like it had anything to do with them, and then a whole swarm of those goddamn security guards showed up. They were all around me and told me not to move or anything, like I was fucking armed or something, and there were people gathered around Andrea so I couldn't see her. The security guards took me over the bridge, down the escalators, past the fountain, into this little office and sat me down there and the same guy who had given us a hard time before asked me for some identification and asked me what the hell I thought I was doing. I said there had been an accident and he said, *There sure as hell has been!* and then a couple police officers showed up—like they don't have anything better to do in the middle of fucking Boston—and one of them asked me what had happened and I said, *An accident,* and he asked if I liked to beat my girlfriends up and I said, *No sir!* and he asked if I broke collarbones for kicks, all with that real thick accent only the police officers and the guys who drive the ComElectric trucks have. I was burning right then, only a different kind of anger than before, and one of the cops frisked me and found the Old Crow and snickered at me before throwing it into the garbage can and the other cop talked with the asshole security guard for a while. Then they all came over and told me that I was going to leave Copley and never show my face here again and the cop who tossed my bourbon into the trash asked if I understood and I said, *Yeah,* and he said, *No, do you understand!* and I said, *Yes!* and they walked me out of the mall, not across the bridge but through the south entrance. I half expected to see her whole family standing there, her father and mother and her big brother with his jackhammer and her other brothers and a whole bunch of young Chilean men wearing knit caps and sweaters and a cluster of priests, and I figured the cops had known that Andrea wouldn't press charges because she was probably an illegal alien and I wondered how she was going to pay a doctor if she had to get her shoulder set and I shook my head and thought of my old man waiting outside for me, how he would have beaten my ass, but when I got to the doors of the mall there wasn't anyone with that same kind of skin as Andrea's in sight, just couples walking around and teenagers with their noses pierced and people carrying takeout boxes from the pizzeria over on the second level.

I was fucked up for a while after that, right through the summer—just drank bourbon in my apartment at night and kept to myself. It got harder and harder to get up in the morning and finally Jeff called and apparently fired me, only I was real drunk and didn't remember. So the next day came around and I managed to roll out of bed and drag my ass to work, only to walk in the store and have Jeff lose his shit. He thought I was going to beat him up or something, started screaming at me to get out of the store, had Bill, this retard from Medford—couldn't sell a futon if he had lived in Japan—call the fucking cops. I got real pissed that Jeff didn't trust me but I kept my cool and left the store without making a scene.

That same night, I got more drunk than usual and maybe because I was feeling antsy, I think on account of getting fired, I went for a walk. There isn't much going on in Jamaica Plain at night so I took the T over to Newbury Street. I had a shot of Beam at Daisy Buchanan's, had a scotch and soda at Ciao Bella, then another shot of Beam, then another scotch and soda. I wanted to pass out; that's what I was drinking for. I wanted an oblivion. By the time I stumbled into Dario's I was really messed up and I think I asked the hostess there if she wanted to screw in the alley, something stupid like that—an obvious joke, only everyone around me was too busy acting sophisticated to laugh—and then some manager walked up and told me to leave. Back on the street I walked around a little bit but it was hard, on account of being so plastered, and right in front of the Urban Outfitters' windows I saw my face reflected and it was one of those weird moments when you become aware of yourself looking at yourself, so that you feel trapped in a maze almost, and I was looking at my face, which had gotten all puffy at some point over the last year or so on account of all my drinking, and when I finally turned away from the window I saw Andrea, walking right toward me.

She was arm in arm with some guy with black hair and a goatee and it wouldn't have been real, it would have just been a dream, if she had kept on walking, but she saw me and her face dropped, her green eyes bugging out, like I had crawled out of a grave or something. I staggered in her direction just because I wanted to see her up close and make sure she was doing okay, but her boyfriend or whatever he was cut me off; he started pushing me back, screaming at me in Spanish. Normally I would have knocked his head off, but I wasn't angry or anything. Then he punched me in the mouth hard and I felt this rush of adrenaline and I pulled out my knife, the one she had given me, only real slowly, on account of being drunk, and took a swing at him.

I missed badly, lost my balance, and fell face first onto the pavement. When I tried to stand up I felt a knee in my back, and it was only when they were cuffing me, only when I heard them screaming at me to stop moving, that I realized I was being arrested.

I don't remember being in the squad car, or arriving at the station. When I came to I was in a holding cell and I was cold. I had vomited on myself. A cop came by, said I had been charged with first-degree assault, resisting arrest, and public intoxication. I had to call my mom to bail me out. She had been worried about me, said I hadn't sounded like myself on the phone lately, which weirded me out, since I didn't recall having spoken to her at all in the last month or so.

When my mom picked me up the next day I had her drive me back to my place in Jamaica Plain but I didn't invite her up because I didn't want her to see what a mess my apartment was. I said goodbye to her in the car and she said she didn't know what she should do and I told her not to worry about me and that I'd visit her sometime soon and she hugged me and told me I was all she had left and I waved to her as she drove off and once I was inside my building I found an eviction notice on my door. I called my landlord; he said I owed him two months rent. Even if I didn't pay him, I knew he wouldn't be able to evict me right away, but I realized that I didn't want to live there anymore regardless. I packed my duffel bag—most of my personal belongings, like old pictures and stuff, was still back in Lowell and the furniture I had was all futon crap I didn't want to look at anymore anyway—and took the T to Park Street, where I switched onto the Red Line. I wanted to get out of Boston, at least technically. I wanted to get to the other side of the Charles, so I headed for Cambridge, and the cheapest neighborhood I could think of: Central Square.

I got a room at the Y, thinking I'd stay there for a week or so, but when I started looking for an apartment I found that they weren't as inexpensive as I had thought. One night, walking back to my room, I saw a stream of people going into the building. I followed them down the hallway. It turned out they were attending an AA meeting. Without thinking that I could have anything in common with any of them, but rather just because I didn't want to go back to my room and be alone, I decided to sit in and listen to what they had to say.

That's how I became a member of Alcoholics Anonymous. It turned out a lot of people joined up in the same way, with a part of them knowing they had a problem with alcohol but without having admitted it fully. At the second meeting I attended, Randolph McClutcheon volunteered to be my sponsor. We had coffee the next day, across the street from the Y at a place called 1369. Randolph was a heavyset black man, very dignified, spoke softly so you had to strain to hear him. He wore a worn tweed coat with patches on the elbows, had a beard filled with gray hairs, and glasses with thick black frames. He said I needed to change my life, my friends, everything. He said I needed to make amends. He gave me a Bible. He asked me if I knew that I was a lost sheep. He asked if I knew who my shepherd was. I thought of Andrea's face, the way she had looked at me on Newbury Street. *Yes, Randolph,* I said, *I'm lost.* And he walked around the tiny table we were sitting at and pulled me to my feet and hugged me—not a little squeeze but a full hug, his arms tight around my back. Everyone in the coffee shop stopped reading and talking and staring out the window and looked at us.

I decided to settle in at the Y, figured I could live a few months there without working if I watched my expenses. I got my hair cut real short and even sold some of my clothes so I wouldn't have to think about what to wear too much. And I called my mom again, this time to say that I was sorry about being out of touch and let her know that I was going to AA. She said she was proud of me for getting help, that she had always wanted my old man to deal with his drinking but he never had. She wondered if maybe he was looking down on me now, with pride. It was kind of nice to think of him on my side, but since he died I've never imagined him as anything other than just dead. Mom claims to have felt his presence, felt him walking next to her in the street, but I never have.

My court date arrived and the judge let me off pretty easy: one hundred hours of community service, three months probation. Andrea and her boyfriend or whatever he was weren't there to testify so the assault charge didn't stick. It was the resisting arrest thing that bent everyone out of shape, although I didn't remember resisting, just being really drunk (not that anyone would have cared for the distinction). Randolph was in the courtroom with his wife and two of his five kids. The public defender called him forward as a character witness for me prior to sentencing. The judge said she was pleased that I had sought out help for my drinking and that the community service work was intended to make me pay back the state for the resources I had wasted and the social disruption I had caused. She made it sound like I had started a riot. She asked me where I might want to work and I said somewhere in Central Square because I wanted to keep things simple. She told me to contact Jean Marton at the Cambridge Food Bank, which I did the next day. Jean told me to drop by.

The food bank was up Bishop Allen Lane, only two blocks from the Y. When I showed up, Jean shook my hand real warmly. She welcomed me to the team, showed me where to hang my coat, and introduced me around. There wasn't much to the Cambridge Food Bank: a table by the door with a big ledger book, shelves all along the walls half filled with canned foods, liquor boxes lined up in front of the shelves, some empty, others with perishables in them. Jean said we had three tasks: picking up food, organizing food, and giving food away. That day I did the first task with a guy named Paul; turned out he hadn't broken any laws, just volunteered to do his part, he said. We drove a white van around to homes, businesses, supermarkets, and picked up food, mostly of the canned variety. On either side of the van it read *Cambridge Food Bank*. On the back doors was a quote from some nun: *When I give food to the poor they call me a saint. When I ask why the poor have no food they call me a communist.* When we got back that afternoon Jean said I could take off or help them unload the van. I stayed until five, lining up cans of corn, cans of pears, cans of beans on the shelves.

Every Tuesday, Randolph and I would have coffee. He'd always ask me if I had had a drink since we last spoke. He'd also insist I ask him the same question. He'd inquire if I had read more about the good news of our savior Jesus Christ, who died on the cross for our sins. When I finally told him there were lots of names to keep track of and that I wasn't finding the Bible too captivating a read, he just nodded his head, which reminded me of Andrea's reaction when I'd say I hadn't been to church lately. I was thinking of her a lot those days, Andrea. Her face was sort of continually there, not in the forefront of my thoughts but in the background kind of, like wallpaper. Usually it was the face she made when she saw me on Newbury Street, but not always. Sometimes it was her face when we kissed by the fountain in the mall that night, her eyes closed, her mouth moving slowly, but that image—for some reason—made me feel worse than when I remembered her looking at me in terror.

Randolph ended up giving me a different passage each week to read from the Bible. That made it more interesting. He also thought I should be reading other things. Since I didn't have a TV anymore I took his suggestions, and when he told me about *Walden* by Henry David Thoreau I bought it right away because I had been out to the pond to swim a bunch of times and I had heard about him and had seen his cabin, which wasn't too impressive. The book blew me away though. I kind of thought it was written for me. I thought there was another story he wasn't telling, about why he headed out to Walden in the first place. I thought he had done something he had been real ashamed of and that Walden Pond was his penance. I figured if people could read the Bible over and over again I could read *Walden* the same way, so I'd take my copy to the food bank and flip through it during lunch, or I'd read it in the van sometimes when we were stuck in traffic.

During our coffees together, Randolph and I ended up telling each other everything, or everything we could get out. I heard about his first marriage, most of which he could barely remember because he was so drunk, and then his own troubles with the law. *Stealing cars and drinking don't mix,* he said matter-of-factly. He didn't dry out until he was thirty-one and that, he explained, was because of Jesus, who appeared to him in center field when he was batting in a softball game in Columbus Park and told him to cast aside his demons once and for all. He moved to Central Square the next day, and met his second wife—now of twenty-seven years—a week later, working in a thrift store on Prospect Street.

Over the next few weeks, I told Randolph about my father dying, my friends back in Lowell, all of whom were pretty fucked up, and then I ended up telling him about Andrea, which I hadn't meant to do but somehow couldn't help. Randolph was one of those guys who listened, really listened, when you talked, so you ended up saying a whole bunch of stuff that would have otherwise never come out. The whole time I told him about Andrea he didn't say a word, or even bob his head. He just looked at me.

Working at the food bank wasn't exciting by any means, it felt more like having a menial job that didn't pay anything, but it made me feel decent about myself in a way I hadn't before. After a little more than a month, Jean signed off on the papers saying I had fulfilled my sentence. I asked her if I could keep on working anyway, only now I guess it would be volunteering, kind of like what Paul did, and she said of course—that everyone liked having me around and that I did a good job. So I kept on working there and living at the Y and while I knew I couldn't keep my routine the same indefinitely, Mom had sent me some money to help out and I didn't want to change anything in my life, at least not yet.

The next time I saw Randolph for coffee, he gave me my own copy of the twelve steps of recovery for an alcoholic. He said I had already begun my journey to sobriety but that I needed to take stock of where I had come from and where I needed to go and that the twelve steps would help me do that. He had me read through them right there, even though we talked about them in AA every day. *I can't imagine climbing this ladder,* he said as I read, *not without Jesus,* but I didn't notice until that moment that the third step just mentioned turning your life over to God as you understood him and I told Randolph I wanted to try to understand him as Thoreau did. I pointed out to him that even though Thoreau didn't come right out and call his God a Christian one he did say that *water was the only drink for a wise man,* and that *Man flows at once to God when the channel of purity is open.* Randolph said he didn't remember those passages, but hearing about them seemed to placate him some. The next few times we met, all we talked about was my progress through the twelve steps. On the one hand it kind of felt like I had already done some of what the steps said you had to do, like admit that booze could kick your ass, and that you didn't think you could fight the urge to drink alone, but other things were harder to take care of, like doing what the pamphlet called a *moral inventory*. That one, I said to Randolph, seemed kind of endless. He agreed.

When I walked over to 1369 to talk about the ninth step with him I knew I was in trouble when I saw him waiting outside for me. The ninth step was all about making amends directly to people you had hurt, except if to do so would hurt them even more, and I knew when I saw him standing there what he had in mind. It turned out he had arranged the whole thing—phoned the security guards at Copley and met with them, then had them take him over to Andrea's cart so that he could ask her if it was okay if I came by to make amends. I don't know what she said to him, if she just shrugged her shoulders, or even understood exactly what he was saying, but I'm sure she trusted him because Randolph is the kind of guy anyone would trust right away, just on account of the way he talks and how slow he moves. Once we were on the T I felt relieved almost, and I wondered if maybe a part of me had been waiting to go back to the mall and say I was sorry for some time, and if that was part of the reason why I sometimes couldn't get Andrea's face out of my mind—because it was like she was waiting for me to ask for her forgiveness.

I had hoped that it'd be busy when we got to Copley Place but it was early afternoon and real quiet. A security guard met us at the escalators where I had once said goodbye to Andrea and the three of us went up to the bridge level. Andrea's cart was at the far end, right where it had always been. The security guard and Randolph waited off to the side with me, and when Andrea looked over at us I walked over.

"Hi." I gave her a little wave from two feet away. She didn't say anything so I went on. "I want to apologize to you, Andrea, for the pain I caused you. I'm very sorry for what I did."

She glanced at me, didn't look at my eyes or face but just my chin, then started to rearrange some of the knit caps on her cart. She had grown older since I had seen her last. Her skin didn't seem as smooth anymore, it had become creased around her nose and eyes, and she looked tired. I tried to picture her sitting there, by the cart, every day since I had last seen her but it didn't seem possible; it felt like the whole mall, that whole part of town, couldn't exist unless I was walking through it. Even though I knew that was crazy, that's how I felt.

"You scared me very much," she said.

I didn't know if she meant the time I pushed her or when I took a swing at her boyfriend or whatever. Probably both, combined. "I was not in a good place then," I said. Now I was unemployed, living at a YMCA, but I was still better off than I was before, I guess.

I didn't know what else to say, or do. I stood there for a second, glanced over at Randolph, who was watching me. "You are a great person, Andrea," I said. "I'm very glad I was able to meet you. It was very kind of you to let me come by today." And then I just said it, for the first time outside of AA: "I'm an alcoholic, not that that's an excuse or anything, but that's what I am."

For a second it didn't seem like she was listening but then she put down the cap she was holding and held out her arms to me and she gave me a hug and I hugged her back and then I started crying and she patted me on the head and we embraced there for a few seconds and when I felt her arms relax I let go of her, even though I didn't want to. It turned out some guy was waiting to ask her about the price of one of the ponchos they had and I waved goodbye and walked back over to Randolph. He handed me his handkerchief and the security guard escorted us back outside.

It was a beautiful spring day. We started to walk, not back to the T stop but in the direction of the Common. Randolph asked how I was feeling and I wanted to tell him I felt all right, better than I had in a long time, but I didn't say anything because I wasn't sure if maybe I'd start to cry again. I wanted to say something, though, as a way of thanking him, and just like that the last few sentences of *Walden* popped into my mind. They're my favorite lines in the book, maybe because they're so hopeful, so I said them aloud, even imitating the deep voice that Randolph would use when reciting Scripture. *The light which puts out our eyes is darkness to us. Only that day dawns to which we are awake. There is more day to dawn. The sun is but a morning star.*

We walked around the Common for a while. The flowers were starting to bloom and Randolph could identify all of the different kinds. He pointed them out to me one by one and then we sat down on a bench and watched the kids scream and wave from that boat they have that is painted like a swan and floats around on the pond. We watched the boat for some time without saying anything. It was real warm by then and I could feel my legs sweating in my jeans. While we were walking down Charles Street to catch the T at Mass General, it occurred to me that I hadn't been on this side of the river in a while. Since moving to the Y, I hadn't really been out of Cambridge, and I realized that at some point in the not-so-distant future I'd have to get a job and move out of the Y, and probably out of Central Square as well. I wondered how that'd feel, starting over again. The trick, I had already learned, wasn't knowing what you should do but *how* to do what you should do; that was the hard part. On the T, Randolph took out his Bible and began to read and I stared out the window as we crossed the river, speckled with white sails, the sun glimmering against the current. Then the rails took us off the bridge and underground, our car screeching loudly as we left the daylight behind.

The
Surprising
Weight
of the
Body's
Organs

Sharon Mackaney was short and robust, with exceptionally long toes that buckled—she thought—like seashells, and black, graying hair that hung all the way down her back in thin, unwrinkled strands. Boarding a plane to Cleveland one morning in late June, the straps of her black purse and carry-on looped over her shoulder, the red Coleman cooler held in front of her firmly with both hands, Sharon wore a pale blue sundress and leather sandals with thick rubber soles that displayed her majestic feet as if they were statuary set on pedestals. Her hair was held in place by a maroon-colored headband that in no way matched her outfit but was the only headband she owned with teeth firm enough to hug her scalp in spite of the inevitable shifting of her locks. Sharon's hair was so long it could only be washed with great effort, and imperfectly, unless someone were to stand behind her and help her rinse out the shampoo by folding the strands over a forearm, or weaving them through outstretched fingers. But no one had helped Sharon wash her hair since it had reached the small of her back, so she had grown accustomed to sitting down in the bathtub as she had that morning, her chin buried in her neck, with her hair spread out in front of her, while water from the showerhead streamed over her brow and shoulders.

"You got beers for everyone in that thing, darling?" A businessman seated across from her in first class winked at the cooler while Sharon swept her hair out of the aisle and began to fit the specially made safety harness around the window seat to secure the hard plastic, insulated container next to her. He had the familiar jowls of the frequent traveler, a large brown cowboy hat on his lap, and a melodious southern accent.

"No, just a liver, Tex," Sharon said. She tugged her battered copy of *Gray's Anatomy* out from her carry-on and opened it up to the section she studied the most frequently, the one devoted to vertebrate organs. The man held his expression in place, unsure if Sharon was being snide or playful, and waited for her to elaborate, but Sharon didn't feel like elaborating. She had a hangover from the night before but that didn't matter; she just didn't enjoy speaking on airplanes. Sharon felt that the pleasure of being above the earth, of hearing the hum of the turbines, of experiencing the pressure of gravity, was best enjoyed in silence. So for the entire flight she read her book, looking up only to order a ginger ale and confirm her vegetarian meal when the flight attendant walked by shortly after they had achieved cruising altitude.

In Cleveland, Sharon made her drop at the clinic, then called Stew from the main lobby to confirm that she didn't have a pickup in the area.

"You're done there," he said. "But there's a pancreas in Miami with your name on it." As Stew spoke, Sharon could hear him puffing and panting as he walked up the stairs from the basement, where his office was, to the first floor of their split-level. Whenever he was on the phone, Stew liked to stand in front of the air-conditioning unit mounted in their living room window, in the vain hope that its white-noise effect would drown out the steady issue of his chronic flatulence. But it never did, and Sharon could hear his ass percolating like a coffee pot as he spoke.

"Where are we going, Mr. Pancreas and I?" she asked.

"Phoenix."

"And then?"

"That's all that's on the docket for now. Well, we *might* have an infant kidney down here tomorrow—"

"Where's it needed?"

"Wichita. But don't get your hopes up: odds of a match between the donor and recipient don't look good, and they've got someone in-house anyway. If he can't do it, I told them I'd take it."

"I'm sure the first-class cabin would be thrilled to have someone with your condition on board."

Stew paused. "You know, Sharon, there are things you could say that would make me feel better about myself, rather than worse. Like, 'Thanks for handling all my flight arrangements for me—'"

"Don't be such a pussy, Stew." She wanted to hang up right then but she didn't.

"I feel anger as well," he went on. "Not just about Matthew. I feel anger that you have become so consumed by all of this. That's why I surf those Russian bride Web sites. Granted, I want a reaction out of you, but I don't dump all of my anger on you."

"Go ahead and dump, Stew. I can take it. Dump away." She found it indecent of him to mention their son's name in the context of Internet smut. It appalled her how he said anything that came to mind; it disgusted her how he let so much out. "By the way, you might want to warn your Russian bride of the smells that await her on these shores."

"Sharon!"

She hated the way he'd say her name, as if he were a schoolteacher, scolding her for some miniscule infraction. She held the phone in her hand, waiting for him to repeat her name, now with a question mark following it—her cue to hang up—but he didn't.

"Try not to punch anyone in the mouth," he said instead. "If one airline kicks you off its plane, everyone else knows about it."

There had been one incident a year ago when Sharon had shoved aside a flight attendant, but no charges had been filed. She had been in a hurry to deliver a kidney, that was all. Stew knew this. He was just baiting her.

"Is there anything else?"

He paused. "I love you," he said softly.

Sharon's teeth clamped together. She felt the blood rush to her fingers as she squeezed the phone's receiver tightly.

"Sharon?"

That was her cue. She hung up.

Sharon took a cab to the Cleveland airport, then flew to O'Hare in the hopes of catching the last flight of the day to Miami, only her plane was late and she missed her connection. She took a room in the airport Hilton that rose out of the main terminal, dropped her bag, and placed her empty cooler on the bed. She went into the bathroom to comb out her hair and brush her teeth. Then she took the elevator down to the airport terminal. At the nearest bar she ordered a hamburger and a dirty martini with extra olives.

"That is some *looong* hair." A man seated next to her turned slightly on his stool and bobbed his head.

"Get lost, fatso," she replied.

He picked up his drink and moved to the end of the bar. Sharon ate her burger, drank her martini, then ordered another one. In the meantime, a smallish man, with an oversized carry-on, dragged himself up to the bar and ordered a light beer. He had a measly build, cheap suit, and big glasses. He looked over at her. His thin hair was stringy and dripping with sweat and there was also perspiration on his nose and under his eyes.

"Long day of traveling?" He waved half apologetically, making sure that he displayed his wedding ring.

Sharon appreciated the gesture. The world needed more harmless schleps. "Not as long as some."

He held out his hand. "Martin Ribbles."

Sharon shook his hand but didn't say her name. You couldn't be too careful. He fumbled with a large manila folder that he had withdrawn from his briefcase. "Just had to gather some depositions for a case my firm is working on," he said, pushing his glasses up on his nose.

"I had to get a liver over to the Cleveland Clinic." She lit a cigarette and inhaled deeply, drawing the smoke into her lungs and stomach, then out through her mouth and nose. Carcinogens now swam, she knew, in her veins, sucking oxygen out of her blood and spreading carbon monoxide into her bladder, kidney, pancreas, liver, and cervix, while tar worked its way into her bronchi.

The man nodded. They both took a sip of their drinks. "How do you transport a liver?" he asked.

"In a cooler."

"How do they pack it?"

"Carefully," she shrugged. "I don't put it in or take it out, I just move it from one place to another."

He accepted the information with another nod. They were both silent for several seconds.

"The average adult liver weighs three pounds," she said. "That makes it the largest internal organ in the human body."

"You don't say."

People knew next to nothing about their internal organs, they just took for granted that they worked, so Sharon regarded it as her personal responsibility, whenever she struck up a conversation with a stranger, to mention a fact or two about the body's interior. She sucked on the olive at the bottom of her surprisingly empty martini glass. She wasn't in the mood, she realized now, to sit in a bar. Some nights she would drink and smoke and—admittedly—prompt a man here and there to approach her, just so she could have the satisfaction of telling him to beat it. Not tonight, though. She rose to her feet and smoothed out her dress. To hide the weight she had put on during the last three years, since Matthew had died and she and Stew had begun their unique, family-run enterprise, Sharon had taken to wearing sundresses in the spring and summer, usually with a shawl, as she had a tendency to feel cool on flights, and oversized sweaters and long skirts in the fall and winter. Regardless of the time of year, she always had color in her face because she visited tanning salons regularly. Shortly after Matthew's death, Sharon briefly saw a grief counselor, and while the sessions had not gone particularly well, among the woman's better recommendations was her proposal that Sharon give tanning beds a try. "The bright lights might make you feel better," the woman explained. Sharon found that she responded favorably to self-imposed radiation, although not because of the light. Sharon liked the sensation of her body being encased in heat. With her eyes closed, and the small, green plastic goggles nestled in her sockets, she enjoyed picturing the sweat glands in her dermis opening while her body shed a fraction of its mass, her skin tissue drying out, a little like bread in a toaster.

"It was nice talking to you," Martin Ribbles said. He gave her a stupid-looking smile. Sharon turned and walked out of the bar. She did not consider herself to be particularly attractive, but men smiled at her stupidly all of the time. She thought this might be because of her rounded figure and short stature, which maybe lent her a slightly maternal air. There was also her hair, the length of which some men oddly interpreted as an open invitation to conversation. One thing she had noticed since spending a lot of time in airports: male business travelers were desperate to chat. They were all lonely and bored, which struck Sharon as interesting because she—in contrast—always felt enlivened in airports. She liked the bustle and crowds, the sense of anonymity, and she had no dread of security screenings, since her status as an organ transporter exempted her from long lines and—usually—x-ray wands, even in the post-9/11 world. Sharon never felt a need to talk to others; she'd share a few words at the end of the day, but only if she was having a drink, which meant that she wasn't carrying an organ. She never drank when she was transporting: not only because it was unprofessional, but also because she didn't have the time to linger in airport bars. When she was carrying, Sharon was either on a plane or on the move and that was when she was most content—when she had something in her possession that needed to be someplace else. The other times she was not very content at all. Actually, Sharon Mackaney only felt fully functioning when she had an extra organ on hand.

———————

Sharon did her pancreas pickup in Miami and was in Phoenix by the early afternoon. She phoned Stew from the airport. There were plenty of direct flights from Phoenix to Houston but she had already decided, if there wasn't another job, that she would stay in the area for a night or two: get a room at the Biltmore, maybe play a round of golf. Sharon loved golf. She had discovered the sport in the immediate wake of Matthew's death. She didn't like to putt really, or use a sand wedge or any of the irons in her rental bags, but Sharon loved to tee up the ball, even when it was on the fairway, and smack the hell out of it with an oversized driver, preferably a Big Bertha. She liked the sound the face of the club made when it pummeled the side of the ball, and she loved watching it fly through the air, regardless of whether it was headed toward the green.

"How are you doing?" Stew asked.

"I'm super!" she replied.

"Sharon!"

She prepared to disconnect him but he changed course more quickly than usual.

"They need an infant kidney in Denver and there's one over at Mayo. There's a flight to St. Louis you should be able to catch: TWA. You'll have twenty minutes there to make the connection to Rochester."

Infant kidneys were Sharon's thing. That was what she was all about. "No problem," she said, checking her watch.

"I'm thinking of putting a deposit down on a lovely woman from Kuznetskaya. That's a mining town in Siberia. She says she grew up smelling sulfur and no odor bothers her. She lives in Minsk now."

"I don't have time for this crap, Stew. Bring over her whole goddamn family, I don't care; they can live in the basement."

She hung up the phone and was on her way.

———————————

"So what's with the hair?" the bartender asked. Sharon was drunk in the lobby bar of the downtown Sheraton in Rochester, Minnesota. Either Stew or the hospital coordinator had fucked up; the kidney wasn't going to be extracted and ready for transport until the next morning. She had busted her hump to get there and now she had a night to kill; this had all happened before.

"What do you mean?"

The bartender dried a beer glass with a dishcloth. "What I mean is, a woman your age, she grows out her hair like you have for a reason."

Sharon nodded thoughtfully. She weighed the pros and cons of cutting the bullshit for a minute and leveling with this guy. Pros: she liked being honest with bartenders; she was old-fashioned that way. Besides, sometimes it resulted in a free drink. Cons: opening up meant breaking apart the hard shell that she had allowed to build up around her over the previous three years, and Sharon wasn't sure if that was a good idea. She liked to think of herself as fully contained within her body—encased from, and immune to, the world that surrounded her.

"I'll shut my mouth." The bartender put the cleaned glass on the rack above the bar and refilled the plastic bowl in front of Sharon with peanuts.

"It was long to begin with," Sharon said. "Then I stopped cutting it altogether when my son died of kidney failure. I was having the same dream over and over: my hair has fallen out so I'm light as a balloon and floating up into the sky, and finally into the ozone layer, where I burn up. The logic in the dream is that, without long hair, I'm too light to stay on the earth, see? So I started growing it out to stay tethered to the ground. That's what I told myself." Sharon took a long sip of her drink. The bartender was listening intently. "But I don't believe that explanation anymore. Now I think that I let it grow just because I didn't want to face my hairdresser, who knew Matth . . . my son. And because I haven't had it cut it since he died, now I feel like it would be a sign that I'm forgetting him, or failing to grieve his . . . passing, if . . ."

She sniffled and then a cry shot out of her mouth, as if someone had dropped a glass vase on the floor and startled her. The bartender handed her a napkin and she blew her nose loudly before letting herself slide off the stool, onto her regal feet.

"I still get it sometimes, the dream," she said, fumbling with her billfold.

"The drink's on me," the bartender said.

She smiled at him without parting her lips, put her billfold back in her purse, and headed for the door.

The Surprising Weight of the Body's Organs   83

The next morning, immediately after the pilot announced their approach into Denver, Sharon hit the call button above her head. The flight attendant, only a few feet away in the first-class cabin, stepped over to her seat.

"I need to get off this plane before anyone else," Sharon said. "I've got a kidney in this cooler and I have to get it over to Children's Hospital immediately."

The flight attendant looked over her shoulder, slightly perplexed. "Ma'am, you're in the third row—"

"Which means you need to tell the three swinging dicks in the first two rows that if they put one big toe in the aisle I'll knock them on their asses."

The flight attendant nodded her head and spoke to the businessmen seated in front of her.

"The average kidney only weighs about four to six ounces." Sharon was at a bar in downtown Denver, having already made her drop, and was sitting next to a businessman who had used her choice of gin as a segue into conversation. She guessed they were probably the same age, early forties, only he kept himself in better shape. Judging by his build and posture, he was involved in some kind of weekly or biweekly gym class. Sharon was on her fourth martini and surprisingly drunk: maybe, she thought, it had something to do with the thin air.

"That's not much, is it?" he asked. "Six ounces for a kidney?"

"Not much at all."

The man looked down at the base of Sharon's barstool. "You have magnificent feet," he said. It wasn't offered as a compliment, it was just a statement of fact, so Sharon acknowledged it with a curt "Thank you."

"Married?" He nodded at her wedding ring.

"Separated, amicably," she said; not a lie but not the truth either.

"Tell me about your ex-husband." He shifted on his stool so that his shoulders faced her squarely.

Sharon delicately lifted a stray hair from her lip that, since it was one of hers, was three feet long. "He's got IBS: Irritable Bowel Syndrome. A spastic colon. You know what causes a spastic colon?" The man shrugged. "They don't know. There are no anatomical indicators. The intestinal smooth muscle just experiences abnormally strong contractions. You're supposed to see a shrink if you've got IBS. It's in your head, see? Gas that other people just sit on you have to let out. It might mean your dad beat you, or that you're chronically depressed. He's seen a shrink for three years now and it hasn't gotten any better. He can't seem to figure it out."

"Have you figured it out?" The man winked knowingly.

What was this, she mentioned Stew's spastic colon and this idiot thought she was making herself available? Sharon ashed her cigarette, snapping the butt in half. It was a game to him, asking these dumb questions. He didn't want real answers. He didn't want to hear that her son had turned yellow and died, or that her husband, ex-husband, whatever he was, began farting at the funeral and never stopped. That bartender in Rochester would be the last one to get inside her head. She lit another cigarette and turned her back to him.

"My wife says that the problem with men is not that they don't communicate, but that they have nothing to say of substance. What do you think of that?" He leaned over her shoulder.

Please. Sharon polished off her drink. She could feel the gin tingling down at the base of her tailbone. She spun on her stool. "You know what I feel like inside, Mr. Boner?" She held up a clenched fist. "This is what I feel like. I feel like I could punch through concrete. Now get out of my face."

His eyes widened a little but he didn't move. "Take it easy, lady! We're just chatting. Tell me more about organs." He flicked a drink stirrer between his teeth and stared at her round breasts. "How much does a human heart weigh?"

Sharon picked up her drink and threw it in his face. "The heart's a muscular organ, not a vertebrate one, you fucking Neanderthal!" She grabbed her purse with both hands and hopped to her feet. "But to answer your question, anywhere from ten ounces to three hundred pounds."

Sharon was alone in her hotel room. It was barely nine o'clock. Her encounter in the bar had left her melancholic. She could accept the world as a repository of pain and grief, but its ugliness sometimes struck her as a gratuitous slap in the face. Sure, there were men she admired: all of the doctors she saw in hospital hallways, sleep deprived and gaunt, the man in the 1600s, William Harvey, who discovered the circulation of the blood, Regis Philbin, for putting up with Kathie Lee all those years. But there was something inherently disgusting about the adult male as well, something at work on the inside and out that asserted itself with a certain smugness. And it became, over time, very tiring to face this thing again and again, both in Stew and in strangers, as if every man was required to tell her the same bad joke and she was forced to listen to it unfold, knowing how it would end but not being able to explain to them why it wasn't funny.

She withdrew a piece of hotel stationery from the desk drawer and took her favorite pen out of her purse.

June 28th, 2004

Dear Matthew:

Today I flew to Minnesota and then to Denver. I picked up a kidney in Rochester that they're going to use to help a little girl. The girl's name is Sarah. I didn't get to see her because she's in intensive care, but I met her parents very briefly. They thanked me for making it there so fast. They explained that they don't have the resources to charter a plane or anything like that, so the fact that I brought the kidney down from Minnesota so quickly gave them hope that Sarah is going to be okay. I told them that it was my job and that I'd do it again the next day for someone else, and the day after that for someone else as well, and that I'd never stop. I didn't need to tell them that I'd never stop because I'll never stop loving you, Matthew. I didn't need to tell them that with words because they already knew. See, there isn't really that much that needs to be said. The heart says the important things. Even when it's weighed down, it finds a way. But you know that. I love you and I'll write again soon.

Your Mom

She put the letter in an envelope and wrote Matthew on the front. Then she placed it in the garbage can. They would dump the letter down a chute somewhere on this floor, she assumed, and then hopefully incinerate it, so that it would turn into smoke and rise up into the air, its ashes settling on the trees and grass that had grown up from the earth, the soil of which had been worked by worms that were descendants of those that had passed through the remains of her little boy's decomposed body. Or so she chose to imagine it.

Sharon was on a moving walkway in St. Louis, her second visit in two days to her least favorite airport, on account of its cramped smoking lounges, when her cell phone rang. Sharon Mackaney didn't like to use cell phones. She thought they caused brain cancer and she didn't want to die of brain cancer. Sharon wanted to die in an airplane, in midair, or in a tanning bed, or struck by lightning on a golf course. The minuscule screen on the front of the phone displayed Stew's cell phone number. She flipped it open.

"This better be an emergency."

"You picked up! Hi. I was just calling to remind you that we have that benefit tonight, in Philadelphia."

"Right."

"Well I'm headed out there now. I'm in St. Louis. Where are you?"

Sharon paused. "Detroit."

"Oh. I thought I routed you through St. Louis?"

"Yeah, you did, but I changed the ticket; I was going to try to get on the Orchards for a round, but now I don't have the time."

"Oh."

Sharon stepped off the moving walkway and went into a gift shop, her eyes peeled on the center of the terminal.

"Well that's a bummer," Stew said. "I thought maybe we could get a drink together."

"It's 11 A.M. I don't even drink before noon."

"Right. Hey, you're going to behave yourself tonight, right?"

"I'm going to do what's needed. Unless you want to make the speech?"

"That's okay." He was huffing and puffing. "All right, then. I'll see you in Philly."

"See you in Philly."

Sharon snapped her phone shut, picked up a magazine, and stood in the corner of the shop. A few minutes passed before an overweight man walked by hurriedly. He was wearing brown slacks and an orange, short-sleeved shirt. The thick weight of his stomach fought his forward momentum and when he raised his heels too high they would hit the front of the suitcase he wheeled behind him, causing him to stagger slightly. Suddenly the man let out a loud fart. Two teenagers walking several feet behind him covered their noses and giggled at each other, while a woman passing him from the opposite direction looked away in disgust.

In order to avoid Stew, Sharon took a later flight and spent the extra hour and a half in St. Louis reading about the spleen in *Gray's Anatomy*. The spleen is a vertebrate organ, about the size of a clenched fist, that holds blood in reserve. It has no relation to any of the organs around it. Also, it increases in size during and immediately after digestion; why, no one knows. In fact, no one knows much about the spleen at all. Spleens are irreparable, unlike other organs, but most people who have their spleens removed do just fine. Spleens matter, but they don't matter really. They're just sort of there.

Sharon always found that reading about the spleen made her more irritable than usual. This was an organ, after all, that was both uniquely fragile and more or less useless, and that combination infuriated her. Sharon often found herself reading about the spleen on the way to benefits. Sharon Mackaney hated benefits. Her one decent cocktail dress made her look fat and she found the wealthy people invariably in attendance to be insufferably boring and annoyingly unflappable.

She met Stew in the lobby of the Rittenhouse Hotel, fifteen minutes before the fundraiser for the Children's Hospital of Philadelphia was to begin. He held out his arms wide, his suit stretching tightly in the shoulders, and Sharon permitted him to hug her. Dr. Milner, the president of the hospital's board, appeared a moment later. He introduced himself, showed them into the banquet hall, and then ushered them up to the front of the room, where a podium and microphone were set on a small stage. Sharon and Stew ate their dinner with the members of the board, all of whom were of such high society that they never so much as flinched whenever Stew farted.

While the attendees sampled their crème brûlée and began to drink their coffee, Dr. Milner tapped on the microphone and introduced this year's recipient of the Children's Hospital of Philadelphia Fighting for Children's Health Award, the husband and wife organ transport team of Stewart and Sharon Mackaney, who transformed their personal pain into a mission to save the lives of as many children needing organ transplants as possible. To a boisterous round of applause, Sharon walked on stage and readjusted the microphone so that it was perched directly in front of her mouth.

She coughed a few times into her fist. "Thank you for this award," she said. A smattering of applause continued. "Thank you. Okay, let me hear from those of you who have donated a working kidney for transplant. That's right, clap if you've donated one of your kidneys." Except for a single man in the very back, no one made any noise. Sharon pulled several strands of her hair behind her ear. "There is no reason for a healthy adult to hoard both of his or her kidneys, when so many people need one in order to survive. You might think you'll feel different if you give one up, lopsided, whatever, but you won't. Kidneys barely weigh anything. We're talking the mass of a couple of small pears on either side of your back. So get off your asses and donate some kidneys. And if you have children, make sure they're registered as organ donors. Think the unthinkable, people. Think about other people dying while your body lugs around equipment it doesn't even need. Think about it."

Her rehearsed comments finished, Sharon was surprised to find herself still standing at the podium. "I had a son," she heard herself say. She could feel her hair resting softly in between her shoulders. I am splitting apart, she thought. I am cracking like a walnut. "I had a son and he needed a kidney and now he's dead. And you all have more organs than you know what to do with." She walked back to her seat. There was no applause. Stew dabbed at his eyes with his napkin and then helped Sharon with her chair. He had heard this speech before, at least the first part. They finished their desserts together. The absence of conversation left the room filled, only thinly, by the clanking of their forks on their plates, occasionally punctuated by one of Stew's eruptions and muttered apologies. Then the beeper Stew wore on his belt began to chime. He pulled out his cell and phoned the number. Mass General had a patient in line for a liver and one had become available down the street at the University of Pennsylvania. Sharon said to tell them she'd take care of it. Before Stew hung up, she had tossed her napkin onto her dessert plate and rushed out of the banquet hall.

———

Matthew's room, seen by Sharon Mackaney after nine days on the road: a twin bed in the corner with plaid sheets and a light blue comforter. Leaning against the pillow, a stuffed, brown dog with fluffy ears, a red collar, and one black bead-eye missing. The walls painted light red with a white border, and inside the border, small choo-choos, all different colors, stenciled by Stew while Sharon had been pregnant. On the small bedside table, a Mickey Mouse clock they had purchased at Disneyland, and a framed photo of the three of them standing in front of the Dumbo ride, with Matthew's head hidden behind an enormous cloud of pink cotton candy. On Matthew's dresser, a picture of the boy's first-grade soccer team, next to a picture of him as a newborn, on his Grandma's—Sharon's mother's—lap. On the wall facing the bed, a large framed photograph of Matthew dressed like a Ninja Turtle for Halloween the year before he died. At the foot of his bed, a trunk filled with photo albums, a Nerf football, a Snoopy blanket, a foam baseball bat with the Houston Astros logo on the side, a pair of Matthew's jeans, and a pair of Matthew's tennis shoes.

There was a knock on the door. Stew entered carrying a cup of Constant Comment, her favorite kind of tea.

"How many took?" she asked him.

Stew smiled, farted, apologized, farted again, then apologized again. "The liver in Cleveland was a go, as was the pancreas in Phoenix."

"What about the kidney in Denver?"

"That one was a no-go."

She took a sip of her tea and lay back on the bed so that her head rested on the stuffed dog, named Doog Doog by Matthew when he was two. She thought of Sarah, the little girl who had been waiting for the kidney transplant. She pictured the girl's parents, their eyes washed out, making funeral arrangements. She imagined them talking to relatives on the phone, reminding them to ask for the discounted tickets offered by airlines for people who have had a death in the family. She wondered how they would handle the reception you're expected to have after the burial. Caterers were expensive, but it's awkward to ask your friends to prepare hors d'oeuvres before they attend your child's funeral.

Stew patted her on the knee before excusing himself. She heard the stairs creak. He had gone into the basement to surf the Web. Sharon remained on Matthew's bed, drinking her tea, while the light began to fade. The Fourth of July weekend was around the corner, she remembered, which usually signaled one of their busiest weeks, due to all the car accidents. She got up. Downstairs, she could hear Stew's muffled cries and anal explosions. Whenever she returned home he would sob for the first day or so. She took a few steps down the basement stairs and sat down. He was seated at his desk, his head in his hands, his screensaver displaying multicolored butterflies that folded into one another endlessly.

He swiveled in his chair so that he faced her and put his hands under his armpits. Since putting on the weight that he had, Stew's chin had become rounder, but his arms were still thin. He carried the extra bulk in his face and stomach and lower back but nowhere else.

"I'm not going to buy a Russian bride, Sharon."

"What a sweet-sounding sentence—music to my ears." She rolled her eyes at him. Perhaps the distance between them had nothing really to do with Matthew's death. Perhaps it was just caused by Stew's inability to control his gas. And why was it considered so taboo to entertain such a possibility? Plenty of people fell in love because of someone's eyes or hair; why couldn't you fall out of love because of someone's colon? Sharon wanted someone to answer that question for her.

Stew shook his head. "It isn't my fault," he said. "Not one

thing is my fault. You should have had a switch go off by now. You should have felt some compassion for me by this point. None of it is my fault."

She didn't know what to say. Of course she felt compassion for him, but what was that worth, really? There were these tremors of rage inside of her that consumed her. It was out of her control There were organs she needed to move around the country and rage she felt at the awful puniness of her ever-precious cargo. That was it. There was no room inside of her for anything else.

She went upstairs, changed into her nightgown, and got into bed. In the dream this time, her hair had been shorn, but as she rose from the earth, it began suddenly to grow. The locks fell down to the ground beneath her, attaching to leaves and blades of grass and even to the worms beneath the grass that worked the soil. She felt her ascent halted by the leaden heaviness of the world, but then the strands began to break off at their roots, and Sharon— now weightless, with small green goggles over her eyes, her body emptied and deflating, her head smooth and bald—spun up into the burning band of the ozone layer, entirely unencumbered.

Haircuts

I tried to stare through my reflection while the scissors snipped the hair from in front of my eyes. My barber, George, had worked himself into a full lather even faster than usual, bitching about the various failings of my generation. This was a Saturday in January, back in 1990. I was in the middle of my third year of high school and still lived—as I had my entire life—in the Capitol Hill neighborhood of Denver, Colorado: a comfortable, middle class part of the city that was quickly becoming more affluent. All the neighborhood kids looked more or less like me: brown or black or blond hair, white skin, bad posture. We all attended the same school, listened to the same music, and wore the same kind of clothes. Our parents all knew one another, and if they weren't friends at least they acted like they were for our benefit. It was an insular place, although I didn't know it at the time, since I didn't have anything to compare it to.

"Another thing I learned in the army," George barked, "was being part of a team—not thinking about myself all the time. I'd get up in the morning with everyone else and we'd do whatever we needed to do, then go to bed. None of this 'me me me' crap. Hey! If there was still a draft, it'd do you and your hoodlum friends some good. The one thing you could all use is Vietnam staring you in the face."

Up to then I had never really cared about what George said. So what if he was a bore and a blowhard; listening to him for twenty minutes every six weeks or so was pretty painless. But this time I was sensitive to his whiny delivery, annoyed even by the way he held the scissors limply in his hand as he bent in front of me and stared at my forehead, assessing the respective lengths of my sideburns with his peripheral vision. A new barbershop had opened up on Ninth Avenue, the anti–George's Place, called Rasta Man and the Chicken. Apparently Rasta Man didn't have a barber pole, much less any clients over the age of twenty. Jarvis and Pat, my two best friends, had both been there recently and called it an experience. Getting my hair cut had never been an experience, so their accounts intrigued me. Next time I needed a haircut I would be going to Rasta Man and the Chicken, only two blocks from George's shop but clearly a world away. This was to be the last time George got to clip my bangs and moan about the demise of corporal punishment in elementary schools, or the communist tendencies of vegetarians.

"And I'll tell you another thing." He pushed my chin into my Adam's apple and began to shave the scruff off my neck. I could smell the Old Spice coming up off his skin, like beetles out of a piece of rotten bark. "The next time I see some teenager hot-rodding in his dad's Cherokee, going fifty down Sixth, I'm going to take down his license plate number and call the cops. Hey! You tell your hoodlum friends to take it easy; there are kids playing in this neighborhood."

Actually kids hadn't played *in* the neighborhood in years.

Kids stayed inside, unless one of their dads had a flashback to his childhood and made them stand outside like an idiot and toss a baseball, but I didn't bother correcting him. I just glanced around his very clean, very traditional barbershop, lined with fake wood paneling, and a sitting area carpeted brown. The couch backed up against the wall looked comfortable, although I had never sat on it. I could almost picture the whole room miniaturized and featured in a diorama, like the ones in the Museum of Natural History downtown.

"Hey!"

George was always saying "Hey!" sometimes by itself, often followed by an unnatural pause, as if he had just received an electric shock. I waited for him to start up again.

"I don't entirely blame you kids. You don't respect the law because you look around and all you see are people who don't respect the law. Like those actors snorting drugs, or any of those dirt bags who sing those awful songs. Hey! I wouldn't even call it singing; they just scream and grab at their crotches, and you idiots eat it up."

He set his scissors down on the counter and regarded me sternly in the mirror. My "George doo," very short above the ears and in back, with just a whisk of a part high up on the forehead, was in place. He spun me around in the chair, produced the familiar hand-held mirror so that I could survey my neckline, then snapped off my apron so that the hair on my shoulders fell to the floor. I stepped out of the chair and paid my six dollars: five for the cut and the customary one dollar tip. Even then, six bucks was an undeniable bargain for a haircut. My dad paid twenty at the salon where he went but all the hairstylists there were women, not barbers, and they didn't just cut his hair: they filed his nails too, and had these special scissors that could get in and thin out the thick underbrush that grew in his ears.

"Our culture's like a street whose gutters are so clogged up the sewage is spilling out all over the place," George said as I put my hand on the doorknob. He always liked to send me off with one final platitude. The tiny bells on the door rang as I stepped outside. I wondered if I'd ever hear their annoying chime again. I didn't think so. I was ready for a change.

I thought about my hair much more than usual over the next two months. That is, I checked its growth every now and then. Before I had barely combed my hair, but now I had something to look forward to when it came time to get a trim. Hoping for a fight, I had informed my mom that I was done with George's Place. She couldn't have cared less. So there was nothing to stand in the way of my first trip to Rasta Man. I just had to wait for my hair to grow.

Sitting in Pat's basement with him and Jarvis, watching *Fletch* on videotape for the seven-hundredth time one Friday in March, I examined their haircuts. Pat's was above his eyebrows in front, then got gradually longer so it covered his ears to their lobes and hung down past the collar of his torn shirt, making his entire face seem pointed and ratlike. Jarvis, in contrast, had no hair on the back of his head, just stubble, while the hair in front seemed to stick up slightly in the middle of his head before drooping down and parting just above his nostrils. One sideburn—on the right—was completely gone; the other reached the base of his jaw. He had also added a gold hoop earring to his left ear. They seemed the victims of hate crimes more than they did paying customers of a barber, but they displayed their new looks like badges of honor and I could understand why; no parents would want their kid to look like them.

"Yeah," I cleared my throat so as to draw a little attention away from the movie, "my next haircut I'm having at Rasta Man, no doubt about it."

"You know, Juma doesn't take reservations," Jarvis mumbled. He always mumbled; something was wrong with the left side of his mouth—it was paralyzed—so he couldn't enunciate very well. "You just have to go and wait."

"How long?"

"Depends. *Last time* I was there," he laid stress on the fact that by this time he had been to Juma's more than once, "I was in and out in under twenty-five minutes. The time before I must have waited two hours. How about you Pat?"

"About the same." Pat was working on a scab he had earned at a skateboarding tournament.

"Two hours or twenty minutes?" I asked him.

"Yeah."

We watched the familiar scenes of the movie unfold: Fletch breaking into his own apartment, visiting a urologist, billing his steak sandwich to the Underhills. We spoke most of the lines along with Chevy Chase. When he was inspired—which was fairly rare—Pat could imitate the man down to the twitch of his eyelids. That day he only mumbled the words halfheartedly, unintentionally imitating Jarvis.

"So you're definitely going to go?" Pat asked.

"Yeah, I'm going." I watched the movie with feigned interest. Fletch successfully eluded a giant dog at a real estate office. The two of them looked me over. "I mean, hell, I've had enough of George."

We watched the movie's conclusion. Then we rewound it and watched it again.

When I walked into Rasta Man and the Chicken the next day there were three guys already waiting. I noticed them before I entered; they were sitting in the folding chairs I had heard about with their backs to the window. Accustomed to George's meticulous appointment schedule, I had never seen so many people in a barbershop before. Stepping through the doorway, my eyes were drawn to a rubber chicken nailed to the wall, a wall covered with graffiti and doodles, all written with magic markers I saw piled up on the floor. I started to read some of what had been written: lots of "Fucks," a fair number of references to masturbation, to other people's moms, as well as combinations (other people's moms masturbating, masturbating about other people's moms, and so on).

"Gringo! You wanna write something?"

At the far end of the room an enormous man with a large pair of scissors in his hand, wearing Ray-Bans, a tattered Oakland Raiders baseball cap, and an enormous Raiders jersey, looked at me. It had to be Juma. He had a scraggly black beard and a belly that seemed to start just under his neck, ending somewhere around his knees. Behind him, a kid my age was sitting in a barber's chair, eyes glazed over, his head half shaved.

"No, that's okay." I stepped back from the wall. I was a little in shock. I had never seen anyone in Denver wearing Oakland Raiders paraphernalia.

"Aw, come on, *niño*. Give us your name at least. Give us one *punta*. Tell us which teacher you'd crush under a flatbed. I'm going to paint over it all anyway, once I get the money to fix up this place."

Juma held his scissors in the air, waiting. The other guys in the shop looked at me with hostile boredom. I bent over, picked up one of the markers, and wrote "Walker Sucks." "My history teacher," I explained. Actually I liked him a lot, but his name was the first that came to mind. The guys nodded their heads and Juma went back to work.

In front of the line of folding chairs was a cardboard box with magazines piled on top of it. At George's I had been accustomed to the pristine covers of *Playboy* and *Penthouse*—unquestionably off limits to minors—but Juma had other offerings, all nonglossy, which his customers were openly sampling. There weren't any more chairs available so I sank down onto the floor. There was hair everywhere, large clumps of it. It was like the place hadn't been swept . . . ever. I looked at the graffiti for a few minutes. One contribution—"Rough Sex"—vaguely resembled Jarvis's handwriting. Who was he kidding? There was a TV right above the door in the corner but it wasn't on. Again I looked at the three guys who had been waiting before me. The magazines in their hands twisted and turned like parts of a Calder mobile. No one was giving me so much as a glance so I slid over on the floor and plunged my hand into the pile, pulling out the first magazine I could grab.

Big Butts was a bad choice. One large ass after another, pages and pages of them. I wondered what I was missing, what erotic intimations were slipping past my untrained eyes. At the very least the magazine was well titled. Some of the butts were so big they didn't look like butts at all. One I could have sworn was an aerial shot of Yellowstone. Another, covered with jet black hairs, could have passed for an inkblot test. There was a butt buried under a fruit salad, a tattooed butt—Cerberus, the hound of hell, his three heads on one cheek, three serpents' tails on the other—butts with women's faces upside down underneath them, butts squeezed against glass, sunburned butts peeking out of piles of sand. I set the magazine down.

"Okay, *niño*. Fuck off. Next victim." Juma slapped at the kid's shoulders while the de-haired customer flapped out his shirt, trying to shake off all of the hair. "You know, I'd keep going," Juma was saying, "but there ain't nothing left to cut. It can't get no shorter than that."

The kid dug into his pants pocket. No five dollars plus one for the tip; Juma charged ten even. When I checked my wallet I found that I was four short.

One of the other guys who I thought was waiting to get a haircut ended up leaving with the bald kid, tossing his crumpled issue of *Climax* onto the pile. The next one up had the hair above his ears shaved and a rat-tail carved out in back. The one after him—his hair knotted and big—didn't say a word the whole time. Juma cut and combed and cut and combed for pretty near half an hour before he told the guy to go home, light it on fire, and stick his head in the toilet. The guy nodded in agreement and pulled a Walkman out of a pocket of his jean jacket. He left the shop with the volume on high, Jane's Addiction spilling out of his headphones.

"Let's go, *niño*."

We were alone in the shop now. I headed for the chair while Juma walked over to the door to flip over the OPEN sign. He was ready to close up and it was barely after three.

"Man, you look like a real little fucker." He put his hands on my shoulders and before I had the courage to mention my financial situation pushed me into the seat. I couldn't see him now; there was no mirror in front of us, just the scribbled-on wall.

"So you like butts, do you?" Juma asked, as he tucked a few pieces of paper towel underneath my collar.

"No, no. I was, uh—"

"Just kidding, *niño*. What brings you to the Fat Chicken?"

I didn't know if he meant the shop or himself. "Friends," I answered.

"Friends. Well we all need friends, don't we, *niño*? Without friends we are nowhere in this world. We are fucked without friends, *niño*. Is Juma right or is Juma right?"

I nodded my head and the point of his scissors hit me in the back of the ear.

"So you another escapee from George's correctional facility?" Juma dabbed at my wound with what I guessed must have been the bottom of his untucked jersey.

"Yeah."

"You think his real name is George? He changed the pronunciation so he'd sound more American. It's Jorge. That's what his goddamn name is. Call him Jorge the next time you walk by, watch him freak out."

"Jorge?"

"That's right." I could barely hear his voice over the swishing sound made by the scissors. He was really flying along, the menacing hiss of the blades punctuated by occasional slaps to my head with his free hand.

"I really got you, didn't I? You're bleeding like a stuck pig."

He poked at my ear some more. There was a little pain but not much. Juma slashed and cut, he dug, he probed, he ripped and tore like a beaver at dam-building time, yanking on some strands as if they were weeds. Then he stepped outside to smoke a cigarette and sing a little. I listened to him wail an old CCR song, then something in Spanish, then his own version of "Try to Remember" from *The Fantasticks*. When he finally came back inside all he did was comb and wet down my hair before spinning me around to face him, looking down at me over the rims of his sunglasses and asking if it would do.

I was pretty sure that I wasn't getting a hand-held mirror and nodded my head enthusiastically. We walked out of the shop together, Juma locking the door behind us.

"So keep cool, *niño*," he said to me.

"Okay. Can I . . ." I fumbled with my wallet. "Would you mind if I ran home for—"

He waved his hands at me, snatching up the crumpled five and one. "Next time, bring some ice cream," he said. "A pint of butter pecan. Juma loves ice cream."

I told him I wouldn't forget. On the way home I tried to get a glimpse of my haircut—in the windows of parked cars, off the glass of the phone booth on Marion Street and Ninth—but I saw next to nothing. It wasn't until I stepped onto our front porch and

Mom opened the door for me—quickly staggering back into the foyer—that I realized I had undergone a metamorphosis.

"Jesus," she said, "you look like a Mexican."

"He's my brother, you know, Juma. My little brother."

I didn't say a word. I was back at George's. It was the end of May. The juniors at my school served as ushers for the graduating class and Mom had insisted I get a respectable haircut for the ceremony. I had protested but pretty soon word got around that everyone was being sent to George's—they had banded together on this one, our mothers—so I gave up the fight. Still, I was pissed about the whole thing. It was degrading, having to return to George's Place after Rasta Man, like riding your bike to school after getting your driver's license.

"I taught him. Do you understand? Hey! I taught him how to be a barber and then he turns around and makes a mockery of it all. Rasta Man and the Chicken! What kind of name is that? What is that supposed to mean?"

I shrugged my shoulders.

"Hours we spent in this shop here," he clipped away, head shaking all the while, "me going over the different scissors, the chair, the hair sprays. The guy couldn't shave a sideburn. He couldn't cut a lawn, much less someone's hair. You think he's fat now? He's a reed compared to before. But I didn't say a word. I didn't lecture him, not about his living. I just showed him how to cut hair; I showed him everything. Now you think anyone without a death wish would let the man come near him? Look at what he did to you! You got some strands two inches longer than other ones! You got scar tissue on your earlobe, for Chrissakes. He treated your head like it was made of lettuce. You would have gotten a better cut at the vet's."

George snapped the apron off from around my neck like a whip. He had taken off even more than usual this time around. He had really been rolling, at least for George, and he hadn't droned on quite like he had before. Obviously, thinking of his brother energized him.

I counted out six dollars.

"His life was in shambles." He pointed a comb right at my chest. "You understand. Hey! Shambles. How many times can a man get arrested for stealing Lincoln Continentals? Every Saturday night, he'd steal the same make and model. Then he wondered why the cops were always waiting for him at home! No, he did it to get caught; he was his own worst enemy. So he lost it all and what did I do? What did his tight-ass older brother do for him? I taught him a profession. The greatest gift you can give someone I gave my brother Juma and in return he opens a shop two blocks from mine and thumbs his nose at everything I believe in, all the while taking away my business. There's appreciation for you."

He picked the broom up from the back of the shop and began to sweep. I opened the door. The bells chimed loudly. I shut the door behind me very carefully and walked home.

It was a rainy Saturday in late June. The summer was just beginning and I was already bored to tears. As usual, I dropped by Pat's house, rang the doorbell, and when his mom didn't answer let myself in using the key they hid behind the mailbox.

Pat and Jarvis were in the basement. *Fletch* was on, but they didn't seem to be watching it. Instead, they were glaring at the staircase, waiting for me to arrive.

"What?" I asked Pat.

He shrugged his shoulders.

"We're bored," Jarvis explained.

"I'm bored too," I said.

"This town sucks," Pat grumbled, "nothing to do."

"There's Elitch's," I offered.

"The amusement park!" Pat sneered. "Maybe if we were in middle school."

In the background, Fletch was having his first meeting with the wealthy polygamist who was to plot his murder throughout the film. A thin line of fuzz was visible in the middle of the scene; the tape was beginning to wear out.

"This is ridiculous," Pat said abruptly. "We got to get some pot or something."

Some guys in our class had begun to claim that they were getting stoned fairly regularly, and marijuana was a fixture at all of the seniors' parties—or so we had heard—so Pat's declaration didn't surprise me.

"Mike," Pat went on, "he's been getting baked all summer up at his grandmother's condo in Copper."

Mike Bikster was a year ahead of us and Pat claimed him as a friend, although neither Jarvis nor I had ever seen them together.

"Grandma Bikster is a pothead?"

"No, you idiot." He threw the remote control at Jarvis's head and missed badly. "She's not using the place. I'm supposed to go up and hang with him in a couple of weekends."

Jarvis and I registered our skepticism by not saying anything.

"We got to find someone we can score some weed from." Pat paused, then snapped his fingers. "I know! What about Juma?"

His apparent epiphany didn't fool me. Pat had concocted this plan hours, maybe days, before, and now he was trying it out on us.

"Why Juma?" I asked.

"He's Hispanic you idiot. Have you ever driven down Pecos? They got pot growing in their backyards. It's basically legal for them, or at least the cops don't bust them, not like they would us if we had some cannabis growing over on the Seventh Avenue Parkway. We got to go talk to him. He can set us up."

I wasn't so sure, but I didn't voice any opposition. In fact, it seemed worth a try. At least, asking Juma didn't appear to carry with it any risks.

"I'll provide my basement, dudes," Pat added. "It'll make Fletch a hell of a lot funnier too, I'll tell you that."

The next day, in the early afternoon, we dropped by Rasta Man. I brought the ice cream I owed Juma, put it in the freezer he pointed to, and grabbed the last seat available. Our plan was to wait until he closed up for the day and then ask him if he could help us out. Any other barbershop and it would have seemed really weird, but guys were hanging out at Juma's all the time, mostly just to check out his magazines and watch TV. So we sat there and waited. When the last customer filed out he asked us who was first and we told him that we didn't need anything done and he nodded and sat down in the barber's chair.

"So you seen my brother?" he asked me. For some reason he had associated me with George, why I didn't know; maybe my hair retained the imprint of its "George doo" more than anyone else's.

"Nope," I muttered.

"He wanted to be a lawyer, did you know that?"

I shook my head no.

"Ma said he was going to be the first Hispanic Supreme Court Justice." He spun the chair around, retrieved the pint of ice cream and the plastic spoon I had brought him, and dug in. "Oh it was crazy, *niños*. He'd talk about the fucking Constitution like it had tits and an ass. Unbelievable. Then Dad's business—he ran a junkyard, dumping people's trash—it went under. Not because of financial reasons—no, he could run a business, my dad—but because some of his workers were dumping the trash down in Mapleton, in empty lots. They were pocketing the money Dad was giving them to pay the dumping fee. Those bastards down at City and County closed us right after the hearing, so Jorge had to kiss college goodbye, not to mention law school. He was in the army for a while. When he got out, he opened his shop on Sixth. That was twenty-two years ago and he's still sweeping up hair. There's your American dream, *niño*. My brother Jorge, the first Hispanic Supreme Court Justice, cutting hair. *Bienvenido a los Estados Unidos*."

We all chuckled knowingly but I don't think the story made any impression on us at the time. We were too busy thinking about our pitch.

"He tell you about being a war hero?" Juma asked suddenly. "Yeah, he counted paper clips down at Fort Carson. Vietnam my ass. Jorge couldn't load a mechanical pencil, much less a gun."

He checked his watch, shuffled to the door, and flipped over the sign to CLOSED. "I'll tell you what: if anyone should flip this country the bird, it's my brother."

We got to our feet. He held the door for us, expecting us to leave, but when we stood there in a half circle his eyebrows arched up. "What's on your minds?"

Jarvis looked at Pat, which I expected, since it was his idea and Jarvis didn't like to speak in public anyway, on account of the left side of his mouth being dead, but then Pat looked .over at me, which didn't seem right. He was always passing the buck, old Pat Matson; he was a slippery one.

"We were wondering if maybe . . ." I started over, "if you knew anyone who might—"

"We're looking for some pot," Pat jumped in.

"I'm not a drug dealer, *niños*." Juma leaned heavily against the door.

We all looked down at the floor.

"It's just—"

Jarvis began, but Pat cut him off as well. "We're looking for something fun to do. Just in my basement. We won't be driving around town or anything. We're bored as shit."

"That's true," I added.

"Real bored," Jarvis nodded his head.

Juma looked us over for a bit. We pleaded with our eyes. The three of us were old pros at this; it was how we had gotten things from our parents all our lives.

"I'll see what I can do," he said. "But don't tell anyone. And don't ask me again. But I'll see what I can do."

"Sure, there was bitterness. There was a lot of bitterness. I worked at losing my accent; I didn't want to sound Hispanic. In school I asked the teachers to call me George instead of Jorge. So I wanted to integrate, what's wrong with that? I was ambitious. Juma never understood; he still doesn't. He just doesn't get it."

George was standing outside his shop, sweeping the sidewalk. I was running an errand for Juma before he went on his two-week vacation. Summer was halfway over now; in six weeks we'd be beginning our last year of high school.

Juma had given me a key to his shop to give to his brother, just in case there was a problem. He had also sold me almost two ounces of pot that I had stashed in the unused gym bag that sat on the floor of my closet. It had taken him a while to find some for us, but that day he had finally come through. When I swung by to pick it up—Jarvis opted out, claiming he had to clean out the garage for his dad, and Pat said it was the least I could do for him, since we'd be using his basement—Juma had completed what he called the first phase of his remodeling job. The name of the shop had been changed from Rasta Man and the Chicken to What Alamo? and he had set up a Styrofoam cooler filled with home-made burritos that he sold for four bucks a pop. He felt a need, he explained to me as I shoved the bulging Ziploc bag into my pocket, to reconnect with his heritage. Keeping a shop on South Capitol Hill made him feel very far away from his community, his *hermanos*. So he had decided to change the name and intersperse copies of *Entérese, Semana,* and *Mecánica Popular,* with *Cheri* and *Juggs.* On the way out I noticed that the rubber chicken was still nailed to the wall but the graffiti had been covered over with bright yellow paint and about twenty crucifixes—some made of wood, others metal, all of varying sizes—had been hung up.

"He say where he was going?" George asked me as I handed him the key.

"Mexico," I answered.

"Mexico!" George laughed. "Is that what he said? Mexico!"

"Yeah." I eyed him from underneath the bangs I had just braided with Juma's help.

"And you believed him! When he told you he was going to Mexico you believed him!"

I didn't answer.

"You know where he goes? I'll tell you." George's broom did a little dance in between us, bouncing on its thistled teeth. "He goes to Vegas, that's where he goes. Hey! With some buddies of his. They go and they throw their money away. Mexico! What a load of crap! Of all the nonsense!"

I left him fuming there, in his doorway. He called after me, loud enough to be heard over the roar of the Cherokees driven by my peers—going forty, going fifty miles an hour on the one-way street.

"Juma doesn't even like Mexican football!" he screamed. "Can't watch it. Says it's boring. He prefers American football, with the yellow posts and everything. He's no Mexican, my brother. He's no more Mexican than I am. Don't let him fool you!"

For the next few days, the three of us sat in Pat's basement, watched *Fletch*, and smoked our pot. Mrs. Matson, Pat's mom, was gone every day—doing what I don't know. "Community stuff," Pat said, "like for the Junior League."

It was true; weed did make the movie funnier. We would giggle and punch each other, throw the couch pillows across the room, try—and fail—to do cartwheels. Then we'd go upstairs and eat a couple loaves of bread, a bag of chips, a package of deli meat, saltines, anything we could find.

We kept the windows in the basement propped open, with the shades still drawn over them and a couple of rotating fans on the floor angled up toward them. And we burned incense—more than enough precautions, we were pretty sure.

That weekend, during dinner, my mom cleared her throat precipitously and my father took her cue.

"I'm not sure if we want you getting your hair cut by the Pasta Man," he said.

"*Rasta* Man."

"Right."

"Margaret Schmidt walked by a few weeks ago," my mother chimed in, "and said the walls inside are covered with graffiti?"

"He's repainted since then."

My father chewed his pork chop with a look of consternation. "Does this guy even know how to cut hair? Yours is all uneven."

"George trained him."

Our forks clanked against our plates. My parents exchanged tired glances.

"Well, I guess it's okay," my father muttered.

Mom wasn't ready to let it go. She set down her silverware. "Just because he lets you write on his walls, don't think you can start vandalizing buildings. You have to be very careful this year. You don't want to have to explain missteps to a college admissions committee."

I nodded my head and asked to be excused. Not that I was up-set about anything; actually, it was the liveliest conversation the three of us had had in some time.

Right before Juma got back into town, Pat's mom caught him toking up in the basement. Jarvis and I thought we had run out days before. It turned out he had hoarded some of our stash. When Mrs. Matson asked him where he got the weed, he claimed that he tried to hold out, but when she threatened to revoke his promised graduation gift—a new black Pathfinder Pat had plans to drive up to Boulder the following fall, when he enrolled at the University of Colorado—he folded like a wallet. We didn't see the inside of Juma's shop again. It turned out Pat's mom knew Juma's landlord, they served together on the Central City Opera Board, and he evicted Juma the day he got back from wherever he had been. There was even talk of getting the police involved, only that didn't materialize, why I don't know. Maybe someone reminded Mrs. Matson that it wasn't just against the law to sell drugs but also to buy them.

I was grounded indefinitely, since—in addition to ratting out Juma—Pat fingered Jarvis and me as his accomplices. When my parents realized that keeping me at home made everyone feel a little claustrophobic, my sentence was silently rescinded, but not before I got a lecture about the dangers of marijuana. I tried the oldest trick in the book, pointing out to my dad and mom that the vodka tonics and white wine they sucked down respectively both had a drug in them called alcohol, but neither one of them would go for it. "I know what Smirnoff puts in every bottle," Dad assured me. "It's on the label. You don't know what those guys might stick in your joint. Maybe opium. Maybe peyote." "Maybe battery acid," my mom added. "It could be anything."

School started and the fall flew by. We all tried to hold out getting our hair cut but without any options other than George's Place we all knew we'd end up caving in eventually. Some guys said they heard that Juma was going to open up another shop in the Hispanic part of town—west of the old Mile High Stadium—but Jarvis, Pat, and I knew we'd never drive over there; not after all that had happened.

One day in early November, I made an appointment and dropped by George's shop. My brown mop, at nose length in front, shoulder length in back, was getting long stares from my recently acquired girlfriend's father. George might have been obnoxious but he gave good, basic haircuts. Plus, he was cheap; I was paying for more and more things myself, using the money I made busing tables at Angelina's Pizza Parlor, a popular neighborhood restaurant six blocks from our house.

I sat down in his chair and extended my head slightly while George fastened the apron around my neck. He started to spray water on my hair to help loosen up the knots, then began the search for the long lost contours of the "George doo." Something felt different and I realized that he was not speaking, just sawing his comb through my hair, shaking his head in disgust, I assumed at what had become of my appearance.

The haircut was an oddly pleasant one. It hurt when George pulled out the knots but actually losing the length felt great and when he shaved my neck . . . that was almost like a massage. Plus there was the silence, which I took as recognition on George's part that I was no longer a mere adolescent: no longer required to listen to him rant and bitch, but a paying customer, a patron of his shop. All told, I thought it was well worth an extra buck, so I decided what the hell and after George had removed my apron and blasted the clipped hairs off my shoulders with his air blower I handed over his five dollars plus a two dollar tip. Then I headed for the door.

"So you seen my brother?" he asked suddenly, catching me off guard.

"No," I answered.

"Well, I heard there were people saying he had opened up another shop. Guevara Mañana or some such thing, off of Santa Fe Drive."

"You haven't seen him either?" I asked.

"No, I haven't." George picked up his broom and held it lightly in his hands. "Growing up he was so funny. He'd grab fruit from the bowl on the kitchen table—bananas, peaches, pears, anything that was there—and use them as a mike to do his own little monologues. When Dad started to lose his hair he'd come up with a new one-liner every night. 'Most men comb their hair after they wash it,' he'd say, 'but our dad, he lets it run down the drain.' Lines like that, only much funnier, I don't tell them right. He told them in Spanish. He was so funny in Spanish. In English he's just crude. And Dad, he'd chase after him to get him to shut up and we'd all be on the floor, laughing, and finally even Dad would keel over too. Juma would dance around the whole neighborhood, needling people, sometimes getting beat up for it, but not caring. He was such a *niño;* that's what everyone called him. At eighteen they still called him *niño.*"

I looked down at my feet.

"I was driving down Corona Street yesterday," George said, "and I saw one of these porta-potties. You know what someone had spray-painted on it? *Mexican Space Shuttle.* You think that's funny?"

I wasn't sure.

"Well it isn't. You know what that is? That's racist. *Mexican Space Shuttle.*" He rearranged some of the combs on the counter behind him and then nodded at me. "Can you do me a favor?" I shrugged and he continued. "Tell your friends not to come by here anymore. You too. I don't want your business, not after what you did to my brother. Don't ever come back. I cut your hair today because I wasn't thinking, because you looked like such a piece of crap, but I'm not cutting it again. Now get out of here."

I stood there without moving. I didn't understand what he meant. Could he banish me from his shop? Was that even legal? I was confused.

"I said get out of here!" He waved his broom at me. "Leave!"

His voice seemed to catch and I thought that maybe he was on the verge of tears. I walked out of his shop and hurried home, imagining George running after me, hoping that he'd grab me by the collar and take a crack at my head, thereby giving me something to use against him, something that would mitigate his anger with a cause of my own. But it was not to be. I never saw him again, and when Pat walked by a few weeks later to make an appointment for a haircut—this after I had intentionally neglected to mention that he was no longer welcome there—he found the shop closed up: the barber pole removed, the room empty. The three of us never found out why George's Place closed and we never asked. I started going to the salon my dad used. As for Jarvis and Pat, I don't know what they did; it wasn't a subject that ever came up between us again.

The River

In the afternoon I jog along the river. I take the steep stone steps down to the path and start to run across from Ile Simon, the small island where school buses take the children to play in the afternoons. The path runs under two bridges, Pont Wilson, which carries Rue Nationale into the suburbs, and the new bridge that does not yet have a name—the one being built over Ile Aucard, where the water treatment plant is.

I'm very self-conscious, jogging. For one thing, all of my tee shirts have English words printed on them. My sweatpants have the name of my hometown's professional football team up the left leg. I never noticed any of this before I left the States; I never remarked that, dressed for exercise, I became a brightly colored billboard. The old fishermen I jog by have their own uniform—blue berets, plain brown sweaters, brown khaki pants. They are not subtle, these fishermen. They stare overtly, putting their rods on the ground when I approach them so that they won't be distracted. Their dogs pay heed as well, wheezing when they bark. I've never seen one of these guys catch a fish.

I thought of buying new, French clothes to jog in, but then I realized it wasn't just the clothes; it was the jogging itself. I'm the only one in town who seems committed to an exercise routine, at least an outdoor one.

I see her for the first time from the steep stone steps that lead down to the path. She is sitting on top of one of the benches that looks over the water. A brown poodle tugs at the leash she holds in her left hand. She has a heavy-looking, black leather jacket on. There are buckles and straps attached to the jacket. There are zippers on the sleeves. Her hair—brown—is pulled back and tied off with a piece of black cloth. Her jeans are stiff looking and tight, tucked into black leather boots.

The wind is at my back. I jog in front of her. I have no choice; the benches face the path.

The cobblestone path gives way to sand, then dirt, then mud, and finally weeds and water. I turn around. The wind is blowing in my face. It is drizzling. It is always drizzling.

I jog by her again. She is smoking now. The poodle sits on her lap. I am suddenly aware of how slowly I am moving. She watches me, smoking.

She is there again the next day, seated on the same bench. The brown poodle tugs at the leash she holds in her left hand. The poodle tugs very hard. *Cacao!* she says loudly. She turns a page of her book. *Cacao!* she says again.

I start to jog. The river is very brown today. There are no old men fishing. Three workers are busy building the bridge that does not yet have a name. They are welding bits of pipe into place with blowtorches. They have tethers that run from the arched spinal cord of the span to large leather diapers that encase their buttocks and thighs. Up near the far bridge, Pont Mirabeau, I can see the red helmets of a group of kayakers. I stop and turn around when I can go no farther. I have a cramp today. For lunch I had a ham sandwich with Camembert cheese. My digestive system is not used to all of the cheese it is being fed. It is not used to the coffee, or the red meat.

I do so little. I wake up in the late morning and study for a few minutes. I shower and brush my teeth. I have a *sandwich mixte* and watch the students walk to the *Faculté* through Place Plumereau. They said that none of the credits would transfer. These are the people who studied here last year with whom I spoke before leaving the United States. They said that class attendance in France was very optional. They said that no one opted to attend.

My legs do not feel very steady today, the knees especially. The muscles are burning and underneath the kneecap of my left leg there is something that feels strained. I should not be jogging. The treads on my running shoes are worn thin. My diet is not conducive to exercise. I imagine tripping on the cobblestone in front of her bench and falling into the Loire. The concrete embankment slopes gradually down to the water, fifteen or twenty feet. My body would probably hit it before landing in the river.

I begin to walk back with my hand pressed against my side. The path gives way to cobblestone. I can see her now. She is still reading. When I near the bench Cacao barks loudly. I sit down at the end of the bench and he barks again. I reach out my hand to pet him and he snaps at my fingers.

I look at the cover of her book. She is reading Descartes. There is a statue of him on the other side of Rue Nationale. He is on one side of the intersection, Rabelais is on the other. The postcards call them "Famous Sons of Tours" but neither one was born here.

You're reading Descartes, I say.

There is chocolate smudged on her front teeth. There is dirt under her fingernails.

What is your name? I try again.

My name is Valérie.

She turns the page. She takes her index finger and scrapes it against her front teeth.

I look out at the river. A man and a woman are sitting in the grass over on Ile Simon. There are children running around behind them, one of them kicking a soccer ball. The light that sits above the river is very beautiful. Seen through it, the leaves and the grass on Ile Simon are very lush and vibrant. A raindrop hits my cheek.

American?

Yes.

I see her head nod almost imperceptibly. Cacao jumps up onto the bench and climbs onto her lap.

I knew you were American.

I'm sorry?

I knew you were American.

My clothes are very American.

That is not how I knew.

I'm sorry?

That is not how I knew.

How did you know?

The man and the woman over on Ile Simon have lain down in the grass. I can see the man's shoes, black-soled, pointed up at the sky. I cannot tell if the woman is wearing shoes.

She takes her pack of Gauloises out of the breast pocket of her leather jacket.

Because of the way you run. You run as if you are afraid of falling into the river.

She stands up, with Cacao in her arms, and walks away.

Each afternoon I am very careful going down the steps that lead to the path and benches. The steps are very steep and worn smooth, each one curved slightly in the middle. The continuous rain makes them very slippery. It is true, over and over again I imagine tripping on these steps and falling, my head crashing against the cobblestones below, everything going black.

Valérie is not there. I walk past her bench, over to the edge of the path. The river is rising. The current that was once twenty feet below is now no more than ten. I step back onto the middle of the cobblestone path. I look in each direction for Valérie and Cacao. There is a fisherman walking, his aluminum rod nestled up against his shoulder. He is dogless. I think that maybe his dog is with Cacao, which would somehow explain why they are not here. I am not thinking clearly today. I slept quite late and when I woke up and went to Place Plumereau to buy a *sandwich mixte* they had stopped serving so I did not eat lunch.

I decide to stretch before beginning my jog. I cross over my legs and reach for my toes. I point my elbows in the air, one at a time, locking my hands together behind my back. I lean against her bench and straighten out my legs.

I sit on the path and stick out one of my legs, tucking the other one underneath me. Then I lie down. I put the soles of my feet together. Then I lean forward.

I decide not to jog. I should be studying French history any-way. I should be reading a book on Charles the Ninth. I should be finding out what the Amboise Conspiracy was. The cloister at Saint Gatien is open until four; I could walk over there and have a look.

I should not try to do everything today. I will go to the library and check out a book on Charles the Ninth.

It is a bad idea to jog on cobblestones, hard on the knees.

The river has overflowed onto the path. I will not be able to run again until it goes back down. Jogging along the streets is too dangerous. Pedestrians who try to cross against the signals are sent scurrying back to the sidewalk by swerving Renaults and irate young women on mopeds.

She is reading again. Cacao peers down at the water that laps— two inches deep—at my feet.

You were not here yesterday.

The grassy bank of Ile Simon has disappeared. There are no more lovers to be seen. There are no children playing.

I was studying, she says.

She closes the book and then reopens it at the beginning, creas-ing the binding back with the unpainted nail of her index finger.

Do you like Descartes?

He is not someone you like. I am getting used to being with him.

She pushes the pages flat with the palm of her hand, then breaks off a square of chocolate from a bar in her jacket and places it in her mouth.

What is he like to be with?

He is like a cousin who knows what all of the buttons on the remote control are for.

I nod my head.

She turns the page.

They have put barricades in front of the steps leading down to the Loire. The water has risen far above the benches. It slaps against the bottom step of the steep flight of stairs I have imagined falling down, into blackness.

We lean against the low wall and watch the river rise. Planks of wood, bits of brush, flash by. One mass of reeds fights the current angrily for a few moments before disappearing underwater.

The town is going to sink. The Loire will rise and rise, washing away the buildings, the cars, the shrubbery planted on the medians.

She has lit another cigarette.

The town cannot sink. Towns do not sink.

Florence sank. Venice sinks every winter.

She reclips the plastic red barrette holding her hair in place.

The town is not going to sink.

The light above the river has changed. It is darker than before. Nothing on Ile Simon looks lush or vibrant.

What would you do though, if it did?

For a moment she seems to look out over the river.

I would go to Orléans. Or Nantes. Maybe I would go to Nantes.

I would have to go back home if the town sank. They would not have enough places at the other universities for all of the French and foreign students who study here.

If this town sank then Nantes would sink too. And so would Orléans. They are all on the Loire.

I would not be able to stay.

I would have to go to Rennes, or Caen.

We go for a walk as the sun is setting. The days are getting shorter and shorter. The sun comes up at almost eight; it sets at four thirty. It goes down without fanfare—hungrily. It disappears with its stomach growling.

We walk high above the river, beside the wall. The current is very loud tonight, louder even than the cars. She walks a few feet in front of me. Cacao is at home. He played in the park all afternoon and didn't feel like taking a walk.

The traffic is backed up along Rue des Tanneurs. Drivers honk at one another. The young women on mopeds weave in between cars.

At the intersection of Rue Nationale the gendarmes direct traffic with orange fluorescent sticks. The cars, idling, emit large doses of toxins into the air. A woman balances a baguette on the top of her child's stroller.

Students stream out of the Bibliothèque Municipale. They unchain their bikes, laughing at one another.

The men are working on the bridge that does not yet have a name. They have affixed lights to the girders. They are using their blowtorches on the underbelly of the bridge, working from a large, iron basket that rocks below the thick pipes and metal plates. We watch them. The flames of their blowtorches glow under the lights. Sparks dive into the black river.

It is very windy along the wall. I turn around to walk back. I do not know if she says anything when I turn around. Above the roar of the current, it would be very difficult to hear any words.

On the way home, my coat puffs out behind me. All of the bikes in front of the Bibliothèque Municipale are gone. Pairs of orange sticks dance in the intersection.

Her apartment is strewn with library books and half-eaten bars of chocolate. There are tapes and a Walkman on the floor: Billie Holiday, Keziah Jones, Rachel Ferrell. Copies of philosophy journals are neatly piled on her desk: *Revue Philosophique*, *Bulletin Signalétique*, *Etudes Phénoménologiques*, *L'Expérience Ethique*.

On top of a pile of clothes by the bed are various articles that have been photocopied: "Les Quatres Causes de Burge à Aristote," "L'Analogie Esthético-logique chez Baumgarten," "Analyses et Comptes Rendus." There is a bar of soap, a toothbrush, and a tube of toothpaste on the lip of her sink. There is no bottle of shampoo in the shower, which is raised a foot above the floor and has no curtain around it. The toilet must be down the hallway. On her bedside table is a book of Chagall reproductions.

What is your thesis on?

Part Three of the Ethics. *Spinoza's affects. What are you supposed to be doing?*

History. The Religious Wars.

Noir de Noir? She picks a bar up from the floor.

No thanks.

Poulain?

No.

She breaks off a square of Poulain and lights a Gauloise.

I sit on the bed and flip through her Chagall book. The floor is covered, I notice, with Cacao's brown hairs. He is sleeping under the desk, near a blue bowl filled with water.

She picks a pair of cotton pants up off the ground and steps into the closet. I see a flash of her thigh skin. Her jeans are thrown into the middle of the room, knocking over an empty Cristaline bottle.

What does your father do? I ask her.

He works at the Michelin plant in Joué-lès-Tours.

But what does he do?

She shrugs her shoulders.

And your mom?

Teaches Biology in an agricultural lycée.

I look out the window behind the bed. It's raining outside. As they go by, the drivers wipe the inside of their windshields with white rags and scarves.

Do any of the cars here have defrosters?

It must be very tiring, never saying what is on your mind.

Yes, it is.

Cacao wakes up. He laps at the water in his blue bowl. Then he goes back to sleep.

We are sitting on the back of one of the benches behind the wall that runs high above the Loire. Cacao is urinating next to a large bush in front of the apartment building behind us. A man is urinating next to him.

You don't spend time with the other Americans, do you?

I don't like Americans, I say.

Neither do I.

She flicks the stub of her Gauloise onto the ground. She looks at my running shoes. She looks at my watch, which has buttons on it. She looks as if she would like to press one of the buttons.

A young girl throws bits of bread over the wall, into the river. Cacao scurries by. I reach out to pet him and he snaps at my fingers.

Valérie lowers her hand and Cacao nuzzles his nose in her palm.

Can you smell me?

Yes.

She smells of unscented perspiration, of tree bark and bench and river and Cacao.

I cannot smell you.

I don't understand.

Cacao smells like a dog. He barks and shits and rolls in mud. You don't smell.

I can smell her breath, thick with cigarette smoke, her hair, shampooless. I can smell the dirt underneath her nails. I can smell the bits of grass caught in the treads of her black leather boots.

You need to let more out. She nods her head. *You need to stink.*

It rains harder the next day, much harder the day after that. We stand high above the Loire and stare down at the raging current. I hold an umbrella. Valérie holds Cacao. It is easy to chart the rise of the river now that it has reached the steep flight of stairs. We count down from the top. There are thirty-three steps to the bottom. We could count all of them the day before.

Twenty-six.

Twenty-seven. Six steps since yesterday. Two meters.

It should make it over the wall by the end of this week.
It's slowing down.
It's not in any hurry.
Cacao barks.
What do you do at night? she asks me.
I go for walks.
All night?
Sometimes.
You can't sleep?
No.
Where do you walk, along the river?
Usually. Sometimes through town, near the cathedral.
That's where the whores work, in the park there.
I've never walked through the park at night.
Do you ever have drinks with friends, or see a film?
No.
Do you have any friends?
You.

She smiles at me. The water drips off the sleeves of her black leather jacket. The water drips off her hair, pulled together and tied off with a piece of black cloth.

I cannot smell her body. She has perfume on. She pulls out a silvery box of cigarettes.

What are those?
Reinitas. They're very expensive.

She lights one with a flourish.

It is warm. Young couples sit on our wall, their hands joined. Cacao looks for a fresh piece of land on which to urinate. I wonder why Valérie's skin never breaks out. I remind myself to check the dates for the abdication of Charles the Fifth and the Siege of Metz.

I look at the cover of her book. She is reading Spinoza. She writes notes inside the book. I cannot read what she writes. I toss small rocks at Cacao.

She underlines a passage with her pen, then flips to the front of the book.

She looks up, lifting her book above her head. For a moment she seems to smile at me. Cacao leaps onto her lap.

I smell shampoo in her hair.

What's the occasion? I ask.

No occasion.

The light above the Loire is very soft again and everything seen through it is lush and vibrant.

What are you thinking? she asks me.

I shrug my shoulders and look down at the river.

Is it a nothing about which you think when you think nothing, or is it a someone?

It is a someone, I say.

Who is it?

It is my sister.

Where does she live?

She doesn't.

I can hear the river being sucked back. It's like a drain has been unplugged at the bottom of its bed.

She pushes the hair out of Cacao's eyes. When she inhales her lips pucker around the thin filter of her cigarette.

When did she die?

A year ago yesterday.

I have finished jogging. My running shoes are covered with mud. The first day after a long lapse is never the hardest; tomorrow will be much worse.

I reach out my hand to pet Cacao. He growls. Valérie pats his head. She pokes his nose softly. She opens a fresh pack of Gauloises.

There are children playing on Ile Simon. Their cries rise and dip, fighting across the current.

Do you understand what they're saying?

I think so.

What do you think they're saying?

I think they're saying, 'Throw me the ball.' I think they're saying, 'Oh, to be young!' I think they're saying, 'We are very thirsty.'

She lifts a strand of hair back behind her ear.

What do you think they're saying?

For a moment she seems to look out over the river. She looks back down at her book. She writes something in her book.

Her apartment has been straightened up. There is a suitcase in the closet. All of the books are on the desk. The bed is made.

We sit on the bed. Cacao laps water from his bowl. She takes off her jacket and lies down on the bed. I lie on top of her. She presses her mouth up against mine. Her tongue runs along my lips and teeth. It seems to fill my mouth. She pushes her head back. I smell the perfume on her neck as I kiss it. When I pull off her shirt, I smell her body's scent very strongly. She unclasps her bra and I kiss her breasts. She kicks off her pants and I pull mine down.

I press up against her awkwardly. I have not had sex since arriving in France. I have not had sex in a long time. She takes me and puts me inside of her. It's very warm. I had forgotten about the warmth. She pushes up against me with her hips. I lift off of her and then push back in. I push in again very hard. When I come, the orgasm does not feel as if it is emanating from inside of me but rather running next to me, like a river, very slowly and languidly.

My body quivers and my shoulders dip. I feel a vowel in my throat catch. I pull out of her and roll to her side.

I am sorry about your sister, she says.

I am too.

I'm going home, she says to me the next day.

Why?

Classes are finished.

You don't have exams?

Yes, but not until June.

So you'll come back to take them?

Yes. My lease runs out this week. Everyone goes home to study. If you stay here, you can't get anything done.

I have a clever twist to put on this logic but I don't deploy it; I don't have the energy to bend the thought into French.

Maybe I'll do some traveling, I say instead. *I haven't been any-where.*

You aren't going to study?

I wouldn't know where to start.

So you won't take your exams?

No, I don't think so.

But then you will have no credits to show your professors when you go home!

I heard the credits don't transfer. Besides, I didn't come here to get credits.

She nods her head. *Where would you go, if you traveled?*

I don't know. Any suggestions?

I would go to Italy, she says. *Or Greece. I would go to Greece via Italy.*

I ask her about Greece. She says she has never been. She says Plato was an idiot but Aristotle was a genius. She says other things but neither one of us is listening.

I have finished my jog. I am leaning against the low wall that runs high above the river. Valérie has left. It is warm today—cloudy, but no rain. The fishermen are out with their dogs.

The workers are not even close to finishing the bridge. They have not yet completed the underbelly. They have not yet stretched enough cables from the top of the span to make the bridge rigid and taut. They sway slightly in their large leather diapers, holding their blowtorches above their heads, sending sparks into the river.

I am watching the light that sits above the river. I am thinking about how loud a certain kind of quiet can be. I tell myself that if I listen carefully I will be able to hear my sister say that she still loves me—that even though she has left me, she is still with me. I sit on the bench and listen. One of the fishermen has a bite. The others turn and watch him fight the fish. Their dogs bark. I look down into the river. It is very difficult. Above the current, it is very difficult to hear the words.

Saint
Francis
in
Flint

In the mornings, Edwin walks down the Six-
teenth Street Mall to Larimer Street and lingers in the natural
skin-care shop on the corner. Around ten, ten-thirty the shop is
filled up: people drink protein shakes at the juice bar while women
push strollers, dropping bottles of calendula baby oil and boxes of
echinacea tea bags into their shopping baskets. There are women
who Edwin suspects are anorexic, the ones who stand in the vi-
tamin aisle in leggings, scrutinizing labels. Sometimes he catches
himself staring at their hipbones or wrists and he grows ashamed.
He would like to say something apologetic at these moments, or
better yet supportive, but he is horribly shy and so never says
anything.

Every weekday begins like this for Edwin, who is thirty-two years old and allergic to ragweed, cat dander, and pistachios. Before he has given up his book for the day, before church, or lunch with his mother—who has suffered short- to mid-term memory loss for nearly thirty years, the victim of a pesticide spraying in the early seventies when, driving through the Texas Panhandle, she was caught under a crop duster—Edwin stops by the skin-care shop. Mondays, Wednesdays, and Fridays are different because he sees Dr. Stan, his therapist provided by his father's life insurance policy. He and his mom have lived off this policy, along with some stock dividends, since Edwin's father was killed in the crash of United Airlines flight 232. The plane went down in a cornfield in Sioux City, Iowa, back in July of 1989, killing 110 but, far more remarkably, sparing the lives of 186. Thursdays are just like Tuesdays mostly, except the third Tuesday of each month, when he goes to the YMCA at three for the OFFAF meeting (Organization of Families and Friends of Airplane Fatalities, or Awful as he calls it).

Edwin begins his day at the skin-care shop because he is in love with the women who work there: they wear blue aprons, their skin exudes a glow of health, and their hair is buoyant and wavy, unlike his mother's brittle bun and his own thinned-out, prematurely gray strands. They're a fun group, the saleswomen. They laugh at each other, toss Power Bars back and forth, and answer the phones with feigned gravity. Always, it seems, they're making plans for their next outing, or joking about something funny that happened on a picnic or hiking the weekend before.

Several months ago, on one of his more morose strolls through downtown Denver, Edwin glanced through the window of the shop facing Sixteenth Street and happened to see two of the employees standing by the cash register. He looked at them for some time, too shy to come in but too overwhelmed by their appearances to just walk away. The next day he saw two other shopkeepers, clearly different from the first two but also quite beautiful. Each day for the next three weeks he paused on his walk through Denver just a little closer to the door of the skin-care shop until finally, in an epiphanic moment on an overcast day in early October—his fellow pedestrians puttering by without any clue, looking over their shoulders for the mall shuttle—Edwin unlinked his hands, clasped to each other in the oversized pouch of his red poncho, and opened the front door.

He established a routine during his first foray into the skin-care shop that day. Edwin always begins by wandering around the aisles in a very programmatic way, a way intended to suggest lackadaisical indifference but that—since Edwin is incapable of being either lackadaisical or indifferent—conveys instead some inscrutable form of premeditation, so that the people who see him on a regular basis usually shy away and make a concerted effort not to bump into him, which is difficult, as the aisles are very narrow—the store cramped and overflowing with products aimed at contributing to the good life—and Edwin's waist is quite large. Eventually, he makes it over to the shelf facing the front counter and, since it is Tuesday, places a bar of bee soap in the pouch of his poncho. Wednesdays he takes oatmeal soap, Thursdays butter, Fridays white clay, Mondays glycerin. He then readjusts his poncho, sometimes tucking or retucking his plaid Abercrombie and Fitch shirt into his corduroys. He stands very still in front of the counter for a few minutes, too timid to look directly at the saleswomen so instead glancing furtively at the shelves of magazines that line the counter: *Runner's World, Health & Fitness, Self.* Then, very slowly, he makes his way to the door, pauses, and walks outside.

In the scene he cannot help but reimagine each day, one of the saleswomen darts after him into the street, calling out, "Hey! Hey!" and he stops, and the young woman points at his abdomen and says to him, "Hey! You didn't pay for that soap!" and Edwin looks at her, his eyes welling up with tears, and he smiles slightly, and the girl apologizes for her gruffness, laughs, and then invites him to an upcoming party where the staff plans to share mud baths and homemade beer.

He doesn't think they notice him, the saleswomen, but they do. They call him *soap guy.* They dare each other to talk to him. Meanwhile, the bars have piled up in his medicine cabinet, on his dresser. "We do have a lot of soap," has been added to the list of sentences his mother unveils anew each day, and Edwin has—with a touch of pained acquiescence—acknowledged himself to be one of those invisible kinds of guys, the ones destined for neither marginal success nor stunning failure. "I feel as if my life trajectory is a flat line," he said to Dr. Stan last week, "ending in an ellipsis." Dr. Stan, by his own description a second-rate Jungian whose practice has been going down the toilet since day one and is now sustained solely through insurance-company referrals, could only scribble a note and nod his head sadly, thinking to himself, *It is true, the world is coated over with a certain melancholy, like pollen.*

The soap jostling gently against his soft abdomen, Edwin turns down Larimer Street and heads over to the Market Café for a double latte with whole milk and extra foam. His favorite table in the corner taken by a nose-pierced couple splitting a plain bagel, Edwin takes off his backpack and sits just up the stairs from the coffee bar on the left, facing the enormous deli counter and cluttered racks of postcards. He unzips his backpack, removes one of his cloth notebooks, takes off his poncho, and drapes it over the empty chair next to him. They're playing Handel's *Messiah*; as usual, the café is filled with younger patrons: retail workers on break, students from Metro College studying and talking.

Edwin opens his notebook and takes out a pen. He is trying to write an allegory of Saint Francis's life that takes place in late-twentieth-century America. The working title is *Saint Francis in Flint.* The book is to detail the rise of a union organizer in the Reagan era from assembly-line automaton to blue-collar redeemer. He is to receive the stigmata in the middle of bare-knuckle negotiations with Detroit automakers, in the process reviving the moribund American labor unions and spawning new consumer interest in brown robes and domestic cars.

As Edwin traces the contours of the plot in his mind it is painful to admit that he has yet to write a single line of the book. Part of the problem, he tells himself, is that he lacks a good work environment: home is too depressing, the public library—although beautifully redone a few years ago—is just a little too quiet, a little too serious. The Market Café could be ideal, but the tables are a touch high, at least in relationship to the chairs, and their near-Corinthian latticework makes it impossible to cross one's legs. But as he runs through these excuses, there resounds underneath them a refrain that reminds him that he will never, ever, write so much as a page of *Saint Francis in Flint.* He parts then reparts his hair, sets his double latte first to the left of his notebook and then to the right and then to the left once more, opens, shuts, and then opens the notebook again before creasing the immaculately white page and then creasing it again with the still unsheathed blue fountain pen that he so enjoys holding. Listening now not to Handel's *Messiah* but rather to Bellini's *Casta Diva,* an aria that so often runs along in his brain, Edwin tries to think of what Saint Francis would have brought to a car plant for lunch. Instead, he cannot help but remark upon the awesome powers of the human brain, how it is able to do at the very least two things at once, and on a more hopeful note he considers, for example, how it provides background music—mostly Maria Callas arias sampled off one of his mother's old records—as he walks through the streets of Denver, at the same time that it imagines Saint Francis picketing or installing a car radio or washing his hands with green olive oil soap at the end of the workday.

Incapable of writing his book, Edwin instead scribbles notes in the expensive cloth notebooks he buys up the street at an art supply store, a store staffed by two old men with hearing aids, their voices scratchy from years of smoking. He has already filled three of these notebooks, mostly with illegible bits of phrases, photographs of cars clipped from the automotive section of the *Denver Post* and the *Rocky Mountain News,* chronologies of medieval church history, Francis's life, plant closings, and what Edwin has termed—much to his satisfaction—"conversion" tables (for example: Pope Gregory IX = Lee Iaccoca; Clare = Norma Rae; Count Orlando of Chiusi = Woody Guthrie; Brother Bernard of Quintavalle = Michael Moore).

It's not easy for Edwin to write anything, even conversion tables, especially in the spring. The last week has seen record high mold counts and Edwin doesn't want to mix his allergy medication with his antidepressants, so the choice is either to sniffle or kill himself. Whether it's because of a runny nose or severe depression, Edwin's case of writer's block appears to be incurable. Dr. Stan has tried to instill some optimism, suggesting that Edwin shouldn't be surprised that he's having problems, or give up hope quite yet, since he has never tried to write anything before. Even though he can't put pen to paper, when he's walking sometimes, at night, Maria Callas singing away, Edwin thinks of scenes for his book and they seem incredibly real. These are the best moments of the day, when he's shuffling along uneven sidewalks and the ideas are spilling out of him, although these times are also among the most painful, for of course the scenes he imagines will never be written, they will only be left, again and again, on the streets of Denver. *If I could write as I walked,* he used to think, *then the book might actually become a reality.*

Edwin looks down at the tiny indentations in the thick white paper of his notebook, the veins of glue dried along the spine. He holds his breath, then lets it out slowly. No, it's not happening today. He closes the notebook, reopens his backpack, and pulls out the books he always takes with him on his morning walk: Thomas of Celano's biography of Saint Francis, John DeLorean's memoirs about General Motors, and *The Little Flowers of Saint Francis.* A few heads are buried in books but for the most part people are looking around at each other like Edwin is doing, their eyes blank, their nails bitten off, their feet tapping from the caffeine.

He stares at nothing in particular, waiting for his watch alarm to sound. When it does he piles his books into his backpack, finishes his latte, and leaves the café. Back on Larimer Street he waits a few minutes for the shuttle to take him up to Colfax. From there he walks four blocks west over to Saint Patrick's Cathedral for the noon mass. Just a few weeks ago, as Lent reached a feverish pitch, the twelve o'clock service was filled with worshippers, but of course they always disappear soon afterward, and by late April only the regulars are back, scattered about the pews, keeping antisocial distance from one another. Edwin settles into the side pew he likes the most, off on the left, eleven rows back from the altar. He lowers the kneeler and makes the sign of the cross.

His head resting on the crook of his arm, Edwin prays for the soul of his father and the mental health of his mother. He prays for the continued financial success of the skin-care shop on the corner of Sixteenth and Larimer. And he concludes by praying for Francis's example of self-denial and modesty to work against the corrosive effects of the greedy, materialistic culture that swallows souls whole each day, depriving workers of appropriate health benefits and subjecting them to mindless drivel in the form of endless news magazines on TV and excessive coverage of sporting events (excepting baseball, of which he is quite fond). Then he withdraws his rosary beads from his backpack and begins to whisper Hail Marys and Our Fathers, awaiting the beginning of mass.

Father Frank saunters out of the vestry with a perfunctory but decidedly relaxed air, which Edwin finds uniquely contrite, perhaps because it is so sincere, unlike the showy, august solemnity that marks Sunday masses, the only service of the week that Edwin must force himself to attend. Mass moves quickly: the readers don't bother over-enunciating and the homily is short and pointed. It is only when the parishioners offer their own prayers, something Father Frank permits during the weekly masses, that the service slows down considerably. The five or six old ladies scattered throughout the first few pews cry out, first all at once but then in more restrained succession. "For my dying sister," one says. "For my niece's sick baby," another cries out. Two others offer only names: "Arthur!" Edwin will hear, then "Stanley!" He assumes they're dead husbands. Another lady, more crumpled than the others, mumbles something incoherent. If the woman who wears the purple shawl is in attendance, which is not the case today, there is usually some kind of political jab thrown in, such as, "For the derelict Philistines who make up our House of Representatives!" and Father Frank will wince as the congregation, haltingly, asks the Lord to hear that prayer (*Hear it*, Edwin jokes to himself, *but pay it no mind*). For his own part, he will, in a muffled voice sometimes, try to verbalize a prayer himself, saying something like, "For mother . . ." but his voice always trails off so no one ever hears him, at least no one all-human.

The Eucharist is prepared quickly, the congregation bustling through each of the required positions of genuflection as Father Frank barrels along. Edwin, drifting off, calls to mind that shadowy figure in Matthew, Mark, and Luke, Simon of Cyrene, who helps Christ for a moment as he struggles with his cross before disappearing for good, and it is the role of this man—not Peter, certainly—that Edwin imagines himself playing: a brave man, even bold, but also inconspicuous. He can picture Simon returning home that Good Friday, saying in response to his mother's concerned glance, "My God what a day! You wouldn't have believed it . . ." And then, perhaps just a short time later, Roman soldiers descend on their earthen house, root through their personal belongings, destroy their furniture, slaughter their cow, all because of Simon's meddling. And Edwin pictures Simon now kneeling before his mother, who wails at the sight of their wrecked home—a woman now destined to die poor, without a home or possessions, a beggar in Jerusalem—and Edwin pictures him crying out, trying hopelessly to convince her that he did the right thing, saying to her, "Really, mother, you would have helped too, if you had seen him, without even thinking about it."

Not the words spoken by the priest and the congregation but these reveries choke up Edwin's throat. When the time to take Holy Communion arrives he watches the same five elderly ladies at the front of the cathedral jockey for pole-position and waits for their jostling to cease before following behind them to take the host and drink from the cup. The cupbearer, a gaunt, bearded man, intones "The blood of Christ," and Edwin meekly, his fingers never failing to tremble, holds the chalice, mouths the word "Amen," and then takes a very modest sip of the blood—lest the cup be emptied out in the event that an unseen swarm of communicants have silently followed Edwin down the aisle.

At the conclusion of the service, as he leaves Saint Patrick's, he shakes Father Frank's hand—his favorite priest in the parish, a doting, kindly man, not like the young Jesuits who drop by occasionally, intent on flexing their spiritual muscles. Father Frank smiles warmly at Edwin on the steps of the cathedral, just above the reclined bodies of two homeless men who have dozed off. Edwin dips his head slightly and gives a little wave goodbye—too self-conscious to raise his hand up by his shoulder and so instead waving sideways from the waist—before making his way down the steps to the busy sidewalk to wait on the street corner for the light to change. When it does, he crosses over to the other side of the street, looks down Colfax to see if a bus is approaching, but seeing none and not in the mood to wait, he begins the ten-minute walk home for lunch.

As he walks he whistles softly to himself, Verdi's *Caro Nome.* Without thinking, he has entwined the fingers of his hands with one another in the oversized pouch of his red poncho, and feeling suddenly his knuckles rub against one another he remembers what his father used to say: "If you are ever alone and feel sad that there is no one around whose hand you might hold, go ahead and hold your own. That's why you have two." His father was a very wise man—not smart or intellectual, but very wise—and it pleases Edwin very much to see that not just his mind but his body, the muscular memory that performs its various tics, has made his father's words a part of its mechanisms.

A storm hit the night before—the last few winters have arrived late but lingered well into spring—and there are small piles of snow at the street corners. The adult bookstores, their windows tinted, are doing a brisk business; Edwin watches nondescript men, mostly in suits, walk in and out. He thinks of Christ dragging his cross down Colfax, whether anyone would look twice, much less give a helping hand; and what does it mean anyway, to help someone carry a cross? Wouldn't it be more compassionate, more liberating, to rip the thing apart? *No, that's not right.* Edwin corrects himself, although momentarily unsure why his assumption is wrong. He remarks with disappointment that he is a broken record, covering the same topics again and again. *Men my age,* he thinks, *without friends, or social skills, we do not become cat lovers, like our female equivalents. We become religious freaks.* And yet, the acknowledgment does nothing to temper his mental habits, and in a matter of seconds he is deep within his story of Francis, imagining the saint giving away half of his tuna fish sandwich at lunch, then giving away his apple juice and finally parting with his lunch box, all the while his fellow workers smiling warmly at him, their eyes glistening.

Out in front of the enormous liquor store on the corner of Washington and Colfax the drunks lean up against the wall, shaking paper cups, asking for spare change. Edwin knows that he should empty his wallet for them, hand over his boots and poncho, but he cannot. The latte is his one daily indulgence; otherwise, he must keep a close watch on their financial situation.

Perhaps, Edwin thinks as he nears home, perhaps at sixty-one his mother might have become senile anyway, regardless of exposure to a cloud of toxic pesticide spray, but of course Edwin's mother is not senile at all. Neither is her condition debilitating in the way that, say, Alzheimer's would be, although she is required to wear an ID bracelet just in case she wanders out of the house and forgets how to get home (which has happened a few times). Her brain is not set in a fog; there are just some things it cannot do, some places it cannot go. It is a little like a car with standard transmission that cannot run in first or second gear, so that the driver must instead put the car in third and wait for the RPMs to pick up before it drives smoothly.

He pauses for a second on the steps of their house, pleased with the analogy. He rings their doorbell, hears her footsteps. The side-window curtain peels back.

"Who are you?"

"I'm your son."

"My son's a baby!"

"No, your son is a grown man. His name is Edwin. If you look on the front door you will see a piece of paper. On the paper his name is written, as well as his social security number, which is 521-21-5471."

It is important not to deviate from the established formula even slightly, not for her sake, as each time it's utterly new, but because the routine keeps Edwin calm. If he forgets a step, or cannot recall what he should say next, he might sound nervous, which can scare her. Of course, he has keys, but these he uses only in emergency situations—if she happens to be asleep when he returns, or out in back; but it is infinitely more frightening for her, the introduction, when it takes place in the house itself. Better to go through things as a door-to-door salesman would, on the porch.

The curtain closes. There is a pause before the dead bolt releases. Edwin steps into the foyer, slips the bar of bee soap into his baggy pants pocket, and pulls off his poncho. She lifts it from his hands.

"Do I have a husband?" she asks.

He stands perfectly still. "No," he says, "Dad died. I'm sorry."

She looks into his eyes, in free-fall for a moment. Each morning Edwin's father is reborn for her and each afternoon Edwin must bury him again. The evenings are different; sometimes he will get back from the Awful meetings or the grocery store, ring the doorbell, and she'll holler at him to come in. Other times she will have forgotten him again and he'll have to go through the whole routine.

Lunchtime conversation remains in the distant past, on the firm ground of long-term recollection. Edwin hears his mother recount on an almost daily basis the first time she met his father, what it was like growing up in Colorado Springs when it was still a cow town, before the army base grew larger and larger and then smaller and smaller. She remembers him only as a baby and so he has heard countless retellings of his behavior and habits as a newborn: how he liked to have his feet held, preferred formula to breast milk, would rock hard enough in his crib to send it across his room.

Today Edwin doesn't talk much. He's tired, he's not sure why, maybe from stepping over the piles of snow on the way home, lifting his legs in an unusually repetitive way. When they're finished eating he excuses himself from the table, apologizes for not helping with the dishes, and sneaks off to his room in order to nap a little before heading off to Awful. In his room, he takes the bee soap out of his pants pocket and places it on his dresser. Then, sitting on the edge of his bed, he pulls his feet out of his boots and lies down for a brief nap. Before shutting his eyes he looks around his room. It has changed very little since his high school days. Most of the posters he first put up when he was only sixteen remain, although he feels—when he looks at them—that they must have belonged to someone else. His desktop, as well as the patch of wall just above it, are really the only space he inhabits now; Edwin has not even reclaimed the drawers of his desk, which are still filled with grade school doodles, pictures from family vacations, yearbooks, a plaque naming him Most Conscientious Swimmer on the eight-and-under team at Congress Park, a third place ribbon from a track meet held when he was in eighth grade.

On the desktop, in the corner underneath the lamp, is Edwin's study Bible. Piled up neatly next to the Bible are pristine notebooks he bought all at once. This was right after he had come up with the idea of *Saint Francis in Flint* and for a few days he had dared to imagine a series of books, each exploring another facet of contemporary America through modernized allegories: *Saint Bonaventure in Boise* was going to be about the demise of the American West; *Saint Stephen in New York*, about the effects of Robert Moses's highway planning on low-income housing. Now that he knows what it takes to write one sentence, let alone a paragraph, Edwin realizes that the notebooks will never be filled, that is unless he begins to clip newspaper articles and copy out quotations from his readings, which he has recently considered doing, if only to fill up the white pages somewhat. Just above the desk is a print he bought down at the Denver Art Museum; it shows Saint Francis outside of Assisi, in front of a cave, his arms spread out below his waist, his eyes looking up at the blue sky, not hopefully but with a look of dread anticipation. From his bed Edwin cannot make out Francis's body, as his brown robe blurs into the background, but he can see—as Francis himself appears to—the blue sky above, thick with cumulus clouds. He closes his eyes, folds his hands together on his chest, and falls asleep.

About an hour later, Edwin gets up and puts his boots back on. The Awful meeting begins around three but he wants to arrive a little early since there could be a large crowd. An editor from an aviation magazine who is an expert on DC-10s is giving a talk and Edwin expects—as the subject pertains so directly to flight 232—that some of the people from the old days might drop by. He heads downstairs and says goodbye to his mother, who is endlessly crocheting an afghan in the living room. She looks up, her face blank, before meekly waving. Outside the light has gone flat from low clouds and the temperature has begun to drop. It's a fifteen-minute walk to the YMCA. Edwin slips on his poncho, steps off the porch, sneezes seven times in rapid succession, then heads toward Colfax, his eyes set on the uneven squares of sidewalk, the grids of cement forced up at the corners by bulging tree roots, the contractions and expansions of the earth as it shifts from season to season, those life forces that push up stubbornly toward the sky—he likes to think—and he imagines just for a moment all of Denver overgrown, the buildings intact but covered with vines and squirrels and flowers, the residents wearing loose-fitting homespuns, and he chuckles at the thought of the poorly managed city works budget inadvertently ushering in an Edenic spell.

The Organization of Families and Friends of Airplane Fatalities came into being in the winter of 1989, after the Sioux City crash. Back then there were sometimes fifty, sometimes one hundred people in attendance at the weekly meetings. Television reporters came as well, at least initially, and one nearly interviewed Edwin but ended up talking to Mrs. Stevens instead, which was only right, as she had lost her son and daughter-in-law in the accident. A lot of the victims on flight 232—originating out of Denver and destined for Philadelphia, with a stopover in Chicago—had lived in Colorado. Their surviving family members and friends and business associates met in the ballroom of the Denver Athletic Club, where one of the casualties had been a board member. Over the years, though, as the crash faded further into the distance and the litigation began—at last—to sort itself out, fewer and fewer people showed up. The meetings became monthly. With less and less attendance they left the cavernous expanse of the DAC, moving first to a classroom at Gove Community Center and then finally to a modest room at the downtown Y. Attendance rarely hit thirty and more and more participants had no connection whatsoever to flight 232. They had lost loved ones in private plane crashes in Summit County, or in regional commuter mishaps. A few were even trying to battle their fear of flying and thought experiencing the worst that air travel had to offer might help them along. In response to their changing profile, the members renamed the group OFFAF. Edwin cannot recall what they had called themselves before OFFAF, something like "Remembering Flight 232," but not quite.

Edwin enters the Y, checks his watch, smiles and waves at the stone-faced attendants, and then heads up the staircase. It smells of dirty socks and sweating bodies, the kind of smell that so terrified him as a child, when gym class was a daily hour of unmitigated torture and public humiliation. The meeting room is on the left at the top of the stairs. Mrs. Stevens, the acting secretary of Awful for the last four years, smiles warmly at Edwin when she sees him.

"How are you?" she asks, holding out her hands, which—because she offers both of them—leaves Edwin momentarily puzzled, until he decides to mimic her gesture, seizing her hands with his own and giving her upper body a gentle tug.

"I'm okay," he says.

"And your mother?"

"The same. How are you, Mrs. Stevens?"

"Quite well, thank you, Edwin."

He nods his head, peering toward the ground, and then moves through the doorway, lest he hold anyone up behind him. There are only three other people inside the room. Edwin takes a seat all the way at the left end of the aisle, carefully draping his poncho over the back of the chair. He checks his watch; only ten minutes

before the speaker is scheduled to begin. He folds his hands together and sets them down softly on his stomach while he mumbles Hail Marys to himself.

He stops after only a couple. It's no use; the empty room, the
drab white walls, the folding chairs arranged in uneven rows, it all
has the effect of emptying him out. There was a time when Awful
was a good outlet, a wonderful outlet. It was a little like church;
they as a congregation gathered so as to meditate on a single mystery, a single puzzling and painful event with tremendous reper-
cussions that were both felt and unfelt, understood and incom-
prehensible. What was the crash of flight 232, Edwin has asked
himself more than once, if not a reenactment in some way of the
crucifixion? Isn't that how the event could best be understood?
Back in the old days, at the end of their meeting they would hug
one another and—as in church, when hands reach out and people
give peace to one another, at least at Sunday masses, when people
are sitting close enough to shake hands—Edwin would feel overcome by melancholic exuberance, so that the pain and beauty of
the world would blend and he would feel about to cry and cry out
at the same time, which is a funny way to feel, and painful sometimes, in hindsight. And he knows, already, that he will not feel
like that when the presentation today is finished, and while ac-
knowledging this unavoidable disappointment, Edwin's thoughts
are interrupted suddenly by a memory of his father—they flood
him at the Awful meetings, such recollections, another reason
why he always attends—and in this one Edwin sees the face of his
father, smiling in front of their house while trimming back one of
their shrubs, Edwin now on the porch holding for him a glass of
sun tea, his father still smiling at him, then wiping his brow, then
dabbing at his neck with a bunched-up handkerchief . . .

Stragglers, now nearly five minutes late, slip into the last row
of chairs. It is not an entirely embarrassing turnout but it is not so
good either. Mrs. Stevens moves down the aisle, to the podium,
followed by a portly man carrying a very large briefcase and a
manila folder under one arm. *What if he were to pass out statis-
tics*, Edwin thinks, *or diagrams, as other speakers have done in
the past? To quantify things in such a way, it's so . . . well, awful.
Better just to drone on for a while.* It doesn't even matter what he
says; it never does. No one really listens.

"We're very pleased today to welcome Mr. . . . ." Mrs. Stevens looks down at the piece of paper she is holding, ". . . Mr. Dixon, a senior editor at *Aviation Magazine* who is going to talk about the electrical wirings of DC-10s." She sits down. Mr. Dixon steps up to the microphone, clears his throat, and begins to speak.

He talks for nearly an hour. Edwin pays no attention. There is a handout after all, a diagram of the location of the fuel pumps in a DC-10 with lines traced about them to indicate the dangerous migration of electrical currents on their every side, but it is not so bad, glancing down at the sheet, not as bad as Edwin thought it would be. He thinks for a moment what he always thinks in these meetings, how he might describe the circumstances of his father's death to a friend, say to one of the girls from the skin-care shop while having a double latte at the Market Café. "There is so much we expect from plane crashes," he would say. "We expect the sense of finality perhaps to hit hardest, that the end comes so suddenly, but in fact the end is not so sudden; establishing the definitive passenger list is not such an easy thing. Certain names drift on and off the list. They're either dead or experiencing a routine day of travel delays." And he imagines the girl's head nodding, her eyes captivated, filled with pity but also sensing his subtle wit. Then he feels shame for the way he has endlessly imagined prostituting his father's death as a way of prompting sympathy from some girl on an all-protein diet. As if such a story would even have the desired effect in the first place.

When he finishes, Mr. Dixon gets a robust burst of applause, followed quickly by utter silence. No questions are asked. No one even approaches the podium. Edwin sits still for a moment, having tumbled again into prayer, and when he finishes he makes the sign of the cross without realizing it and looks forlornly about the room. He feels the calm of his antidepressants, the gentle buzz that displaces his melancholy with a form of cerebral white noise, beginning to wear off. Mrs. Stevens is now standing at the doorway, having thanked Mr. Dixon for his time and sent him on his way. Edwin puts on his poncho and approaches her apprehensively, unsure of what to say, and so he thanks her for arranging the speaker, reaches out his hand to shake hers, notices a crumpled piece of Kleenex, and then looks into her eyes, which are bloodshot and misty.

"There's really no point is there," she says to him, "trying to organize things? No one comes anymore."

"Of course people come." Edwin looks down at the floor, at the individual tiles traced by thin lines of dirt.

"Mr. Dixon agreed to speak only because he is on a crusade to change the electrical wiring of DC-10s. Other speakers expect at least a modest honorarium . . ."

Edwin nods his head. He fears that Mrs. Stevens is about to ask for a donation of some sort, on top of the one hundred dollars he already gives each December, and while he could not refuse to give more, he dreads having to return to his budget calculations to see exactly how much he and his mother could spare. He waits for Mrs. Stevens's voice to pick up again, but instead she dabs at her eyes and gently taps him on his arm before turning and walking back into the meeting room. Edwin watches her from the doorway as she sits in one of the chairs and buries her head in her hands. He would like so much in these moments to be the kind of person who could say the perfect thing, or be so bold as to offer an embrace, but he is not that kind of person. *What good is faith*, he asks himself, *if it does not lead to good works?* He mulls over a convincing reply, finds none, and so he orders himself to go to Mrs. Stevens and comfort her, only he cannot. What if she screamed at him to get away, or what if he knocked her over by mistake, what then? Morosely, he pulls himself away from the room and walks down the hallway, then down the stairwell, then out onto the street.

It has cooled off considerably. The snow that had begun to melt during the day is now refreezing. Edwin sees the shadowy figures of street people shuddering in doorways. He begins to walk, tries to reenter *Saint Francis in Flint* but is blocked momentarily by the image of Mrs. Stevens with her head in her hands. He tries again, now with more determination, and finally breaks through: he sees Francis on his way to the GM plant in the middle of February, a brutally cold morning. He has set up a lonely picket outside the gates. A malicious campaign of misinformation has splintered the union and Francis is now attacked by his fellow workers (read Frederick II's henchmen). They lob eggs and cabbages at his head. Security guards steal his lunch box and roll dice for the delicious egg sandwiches inside. Softly falling snow turns to sleet and ice. The workers and security men continue to haze him. Then, at first seeming to come from Francis's mind alone, Gluck's *J'ai Perdu mon Eurydice,* sung by Callas herself, begins to float through the air. Francis looks up to the sky, then over his shoulder. A battered pickup truck has pulled off the road, its window down, the aria pouring out of it. In the driver's seat is his friend, Norma Rae. Francis gives the thumbs up . . .

"Ah!" Edwin's feet have struck a street person sprawled on the sidewalk. "Excuse me?" Edwin mumbles, and then louder, "Excuse me!" The music in his brain stops playing. Francis fades out. And it was such a wonderful vision too, one of the best in some time. Edwin looks down at the man. What is he doing blocking off the entire sidewalk? Doesn't he realize that people must use it to walk home, people who don't own automobiles, people who have been walking all day? And suddenly anger rises up in him. Is he, Edwin, supposed to lift his tired legs and walk around this man after having already been yanked from a reverie that would have otherwise carried him all the way home? *It is when people, even indigent people, take such liberties that we all suffer,* he thinks. It is a curious thought, not like any others that he can recall having, and he edges closer to another thought, this even more alien, the thought that perhaps he doesn't like street people at all, that he never has, that his compassion has been only for Saint Francis's compassion for them, but that in him there is, rather than sympathy, actually antipathy toward these people. Why do they have the right to ask strangers for money? Why are they entitled to turn public space into private sleeping quarters? And glancing quickly over his shoulder, just to make sure there is no one walking behind him, Edwin lets go a feeble kick in the man's rib cage, and then suddenly another kick, and another and another. He kicks and kicks at the homeless man but none of the blows seems to register with him, maybe because of the layers of clothing he has on, or because he's passed out, or due to lack of muscle tone in Edwin's leg. Stepping over the body now, Edwin immediately feels a horrible rush of shame overcome him, shame mixed in with adrenaline, such that he staggers to a nearby phone booth and leans against it for a moment. He feels his eyes moisten at the thought of his cruelty, at the way the anger had burst out of him, and for a moment he feels the surge inside his veins as a testosterone boost of unrivaled proportion, but then another, more familiar rush overtakes him and he strikes his head—very tepidly—against the phone booth. How could he, a grown man who regards himself as a modern-day chronicler of the life of Saint Francis, even if he is unable actually to write his chronicle, but nevertheless, how could he attack a homeless person? And he feels something inside of him break, as if a taut line of rope or string from an instrument had been cut, and just for a moment— before he can stop himself—he thinks of his life as having ended, the life he has led these last few years, a life composed nearly entirely of inner fantasy, occasionally fed by an incongruous detail pulled out from his otherwise numb marches through downtown Denver. But then just as quickly—because he is powerless to stop it—just as quickly he thinks something far more terrifying but something that makes much more sense: perhaps he did not just kick several times a homeless man he stumbled upon randomly, but perhaps instead, after years of hearing of his devotions, Saint Francis himself had come down to Denver to behold him, Edwin Morris, and this of course makes sense because Francis would assume the appearance of a homeless man, not to test Edwin but just because that is what he would naturally do. Only it became a test when Edwin failed it: when Francis found that instead of being greeted warmly by someone who claimed to be bringing him and his God glory he was being beaten senseless by some ranting poser, some violent Manichean. It is all really too horrible even to process, and so Edwin scurries along, not daring to look over his shoulder, but rather imagining the sight: angels tugging at Francis's broken frame, lifting him back up into the clouds.

During the rest of his walk home, through the frozen streets of Denver, Edwin meditates on his feeling of self-disgust, mindful that he should push his ego to its very breaking point, to the point where every fiber of his own hypocrisy has been examined, but in spite of this noble intention the impulse for relief is too great, and so—with shame, but powerless to resist—he thinks of Saint Francis again, now journeying toward Mount Alverna to receive the stigmata, and he cannot help but feel himself trudging after Saint Francis to be stigmatized with him, and he closes his eyes just briefly enough to see the crowds pushing up against him and falling to their knees, begging to be blessed. When he thinks of this scene—unfortunately filmed in his mind by the Technicolor used in 1950s Hollywood Bible movies, so the faces are all slightly blurred—yet nonetheless when he thinks of this scene it brings him solace, even if, perhaps because, it is not a scene from *Saint Francis in Flint*, and so as the temperature drops, without thinking he links his hands together in the oversized pouch of his red poncho, turns up Marion Street, and rubs his thumbs against the palms of his hands.

Arriving home, he rings the doorbell and waits, hoping to hear her voice call down. Instead, he picks up her footsteps. The light in the front hallway goes on, then, a moment later, the side-window curtain peels back.

"Who are you?"

"I'm your son."

"My son's a baby!"

"No, your son is a grown man. His name is Edwin. If you look on the front door you will see a piece of paper. On the paper his name is written, as well as his social security number, which is 521-21-5471."

The curtain closes. There is a pause before the dead bolt releases. Edwin steps into the foyer and takes off his poncho. She lifts it from his hands.

"Do I have a husband?" she asks.

Edwin stands perfectly still, then nods his head. "Yes," he says, "yes you do. He'll be home tomorrow."

Fellowship
of the
Bereaved

Pain comes from the darkness
And we call it wisdom. It is pain.
RANDALL JARRELL, "90 North"

Jared Reasoner flew into Denver from Boston five days before Christmas that year. His father said he'd pick him up at the airport, which in their family never meant just pulling up at the curb and waiting in the car; they would always park and go in. When Jared didn't see his father that night, he picked up his duffel bag from the claim area and went outside. There were no cars to be seen—just vans, buses, and taxis. To get to the passenger pickup area in the Denver International Airport you have to take an elevator up a floor, something he always forgot. When it dawned on him that he was on the wrong level, Jared went back inside and noticed his father slumped in a chair by the sliding doors he had just walked through. He was fast asleep.

Jared shook him gently by the shoulder. When his father opened his eyes, he started in his seat. His eyes were bloodshot. "Hi, bubba," he mumbled, standing up. They performed an awkward hug, his father kissing Jared on the cheek, which surprised his son. That sort of intimate gesture had rarely been a part of their relationship. Standing straight, Glenn Reasoner was barely five-foot-nine, but he usually slouched and that night was no different. Jared was a little taller but seemed more so because he was so thin. His bangs hung in front of his eyes and he needed to shave. "You look like crap," his father said to him. Jared didn't say anything in response. He felt right then just as he had for the last six weeks, ever since his older sister, Ann, had unexpectedly died of an aneurysm in her sleep: awake, even agitated, but very tired at the same time. He knew nothing about physiology but Jared was convinced that his brain had released some survival chemical that was propelling his body along, preventing him from relaxing out of fear that if he lowered his guard he too would die without warning.

They walked slowly to the car. There was a chill in the air but it had been much colder in Boston earlier in the day, the East Coast air biting and humid in a way it never was in Denver. Jared had lived in Boston for six years, the whole time working toward a PhD in English literature. Typically, he had come home to Denver only for Christmas break, and then occasionally in the summer for a week or two, but he had been back three times recently: for Ann's funeral, then—two weeks later—Thanksgiving, and now Christmas.

The lights of the city were just visible on the horizon. Denver would never feel the same again, Jared knew that. Growing up, the city had been benign and boring, but now it held in its pockets so many memories and reminders it couldn't be trusted entirely. It was liable, he knew, to trip him up, to break him down over and over again.

Driving out of the parking garage, Mr. Reasoner fumbled with the dashboard lighter before taking a puff on a half-smoked cigar that had been smoldering in the ashtray. He asked his son about the meal served on his flight. He asked if they gave out peanuts or pretzels with the complimentary beverage. Jared's dad had a thing about food. His parents had died when he was thirteen and as a result he was shuffled between different family members for years thereafter and never knew for certain where he was going to eat next, or when. For Mr. Reasoner, food was about having a home; it was about his dead parents.

Jared didn't bother answering his questions. Owing to his father's fixation, he hated discussing food and disliked eating with his parents, since his father had a way of steering the conversation toward considering what they should eat for their next meal. In the past, faced with silence, Glenn Reasoner would keep right on talking, but that night he became quiet, and Jared assumed his father was thinking of Ann.

They drove into town, first through the drab prairie east of Denver, then the warehouse and industrial part of town. Jared asked how his mom was doing. Mr. Reasoner said not well, but that they hadn't been fighting more than usual. "Most marriages," he added, "they get consumed by fighting after something like this, but not ours." It had only been a month and a half, Jared was tempted to say, but didn't. They rambled along, Jared's father indiscriminately cutting off cars, clearing his throat again and again as he always did, balling the mucus up in his mouth before rolling down the window and expectorating loudly. "If we can make it through the holidays," he said, with the telltale slur in his speech confirming that he had been sipping out of the flask he kept in his glove compartment, "it will be a miracle."

Jared expected to see his mother in the kitchen, sitting at the counter on one of the wooden stools that only she found comfortable, reading a magazine, but when they came in from the garage she was nowhere to be found. In the center of the countertop was a framed picture of Ann that he had never seen before. She was sitting outside somewhere, smiling, her mouth tautly drawn, her eyes looking out past the camera lens. The photograph was slightly blurry and Jared assumed that his mother had gotten it enlarged. He wondered if that was a healthy or normal thing to do. He wasn't sure, although when tempted the weekend before to cover his dresser in Boston with pictures of himself and his sister, Jared had decided against it: a little showy, he thought, and over-determined, as if a dresser could represent how cluttered his mind was with remembrances. He deposited his duffel bag and backpack at the foot of the back stairs alongside a pile of newspapers and unopened letters.

"Will you join me for a martini?" His father took his shaker out of the freezer and wrapped a dishtowel around it so that the cold metallic surface wouldn't sting his hands.

"Sure."

Jared followed him into the pantry. Mr. Reasoner mixed the drinks expertly and then handed one of them to his son. Jared took a long sip. The back corners of his jaw tightened involuntarily but he still thought—in spite of the toxicity—that it was a very smooth drink, and cold. They walked into the living room and sat down.

"So is everyone back yet?" Mr. Reasoner asked Jared, meaning his friends.

"I think so. I'm going to call Dave in a little bit."

Mr. Reasoner nodded. "What about Walter?" He did another one of his throat clears. "Are you going to call Walter?"

"Tonight I think I'm just going to see Dave."

"Walter's been a good friend too."

"Yeah, I'll call Walter tomorrow."

Jared heard footsteps on the staircase. A moment later Meredith Reasoner appeared. She had on gray slacks and a black Emporio Armani sweater that Jared recognized because he had given it to her for Christmas the year before. Her hair was wet and she held a wineglass in her hand. He went over and gave her a hug. She asked her son how the flight had been and he said okay and told her that he hoped she had been eating. She looked even thinner than usual; her collarbones and the points of her shoulders pressed up against her skin and her neck looked tense and elongated.

"I tell her to eat," Mr. Reasoner jumped in, "but she never listens."

"You know what they say, 'if you're a woman, you can't be too thin or too rich.' At least they used to say that." She walked over to the couch and sat down. "Glenn, get me another glass of wine."

Mr. Reasoner took the glass from her hand and walked into the kitchen. "Your son isn't planning on calling Walter," he hollered from the other room.

"Walter's been a good friend to you, Jared."

"I'll call Walter tomorrow. I have plans with Dave tonight." Less had been expected of Walter than pretty much any of Jared's contemporaries; he had barely made it through high school in five years and slept through his college entrance exams not once but twice, so when he straightened himself out—suddenly becoming some sort of extreme athlete—he received high praise from everyone in the Reasoners' social set. Dave, on the other hand, had always been so good-looking and charming—in a "bad boy" sort of way—that everyone assumed he'd end up being successful. Then, barely out of high school, he ended up in a rehab center and only now did he seem to have his life back together. He had moved to California the year before, found work as a technical assistant on TV commercial shoots, and was trying to finish his first screenplay.

"I'm not even sure Dave's home," Mrs. Reasoner said ominously.

"He got home yesterday."

"I thought he might have to work this week. I thought their shoot was going to go over; that's what Nancy said." Nancy was Dave's mom and one of Mrs. Reasoner's closest friends.

"He's home. I talked to him last night."

"From Boston? You called him all the way from Boston?"

Jared didn't bother saying anything. His parents were always doing this kind of thing when he came home: fixating on an issue and then picking it apart endlessly. Half the time, when he saw them, Mr. Reasoner would call Walter Dave and vice versa, but he had never been able to keep anyone's name straight. Mrs. Reasoner was more on top of such things, but she was also fairly indifferent to Jared's friends; he could recall, more than once, her asking one of them a question and then wandering out of the room before an answer had been given. Jared couldn't imagine, with all that they had just been through, that either one of his parents really gave a damn if he had dinner alone with Dave, but neither Mr. nor Mrs. Reasoner was ever inclined just to drop an issue, regardless of how much time had passed. Jared and Ann had once hypothesized that it was because both their parents had grown up as only children; neither one of them had ever had to let anything go.

"Walter wasn't at the funeral, I know that." Mrs. Reasoner averted her son's eyes, worried he would interrupt her. "But that doesn't mean he's not a good friend. Some friends just don't know how to handle death. They're worried they'll say the wrong thing so they say and do nothing, but they still care."

Walter lived eight blocks from the Reasoners' house and still couldn't make the reception they had after Ann's funeral. Dave, on the other hand, flew in from Los Angeles and had to give up a job on a Toyota commercial to make it. Walter had been Ann's favorite of his friends, largely because Ann always gravitated toward people who were self-conscious and a little awkward, like she was, and yet, following her death, Walter hadn't expressed any condolences whatsoever—hadn't written Jared a note, much less called. Jared thought about Walter's silence a lot. It angered him. Actually, a lot of things angered him in the wake of Ann's death; he had been surprised to find general irritability to be such a key component of grief.

Mr. Reasoner came in from the pantry holding a glass of wine, which he handed to his wife.

"I was telling Jared"—Mrs. Reasoner spoke to her husband but continued to look at her son—"that you can't expect all of your friends to handle death with the same . . . what's the word I'm looking for?"

"Maturity?" Jared offered.

"Yes, *maturity*." She stumbled slightly over the word. "You can't ask for that. If you do you'll go crazy."

While still standing, Mr. Reasoner abruptly downed his drink, which had been sitting on the side table next to the couch, and then shook the half-melted ice cubes at his son. "Want another one?" he asked.

Jared shook his head and Mr. Reasoner gave him a confused glance.

"If he doesn't want to get drunk," Mrs. Reasoner said, "he doesn't want to get drunk."

"You're drunk," he mumbled.

"I most certainly am not. And don't talk to me like that. Don't ever talk to me like that."

"I'll have one more," Jared said abruptly.

"See! He did want another one." Mr. Reasoner picked up his glass and went into the pantry.

"He drinks all the time. What am I supposed to do, watch him like a prison guard?" She sighed. "I don't care anymore." She turned her head to the side. "Glenn, have you heard a weather report?"

"What?"

"DO YOU KNOW WHAT THE WEATHER IS GOING TO BE TOMORROW?"

"No! The paper's in the recycling bin outside."

She looked at Jared, filled with indignation. "He has to put the paper in the recycling bin the minute he's done reading it. It can't wait until the evening. If I want to read the paper I have to go out into the alley."

Jared sat still. Whenever he was home, even before Ann died, he had constantly been called upon to referee between his parents in one ludicrous dispute after another, but with her death, having to listen to them bicker seemed like an acutely unfair punishment.

"If it snows while you're home . . ." Mrs. Reasoner touched the white knuckles on her hand very softly. Ann loved snow. The last time she had been home for Christmas it had been dry the whole time, even in the mountains. She said that all she wanted for Christmas was snow but it never came. That was two years before; she was twenty-nine at the time.

"I'll kill someone if it snows." Mrs. Reasoner looked around the room with simmering irritation. "One snowflake and I'll go on a rampage."

Jared checked his watch. He wanted it to snow, he realized. Tons of snow. He imagined Denver buried, the monuments of his childhood erased, and the thought comforted him.

"Did your father tell you about the tree?" Mrs. Reasoner asked.

"What tree?

"You didn't tell him?"

Mr. Reasoner walked into the room with two fresh martinis, and placed one in front of Jared on the coffee table.

"Tell me what?"

"They're going to plant a tree in the Botanic Gardens for Ann. A red jade."

"I told him in the car."

"No you didn't."

"Didn't I?" When no one answered him, Mr. Reasoner looked down at his shoes.

"Who are *they?*" Jared asked.

Mrs. Reasoner began to cry softly. "Our friends," she said, before putting her hands up to her eyes.

Mr. Reasoner watched his wife cry, then looked over at his son. "We're going to be okay," he said to him. "We'll get through it."

Jared looked down at the floor. "Do we have a choice?"

"No," his father said, "no we don't."

"I should call Dave." He stood up.

"Where are you going? Use the phone down here."

Jared walked up the stairs, skipping every other step. Both his parents called after him but he ignored them. This is going to be, he realized for the hundredth time, the worst week of my life.

When Jared walked into the Chop House in lower downtown, Dave was at the bar, drinking a beer and speaking to a couple of women with frizzy hair wearing denim miniskirts. The two men hugged each other and then did a poor imitation of their handshake from high school, a portion of which involved interlocking their thumbs, flapping their fingers, and doing bird-chirp noises. The women standing on either side of Dave laughed when they made the chirping noise. They were both staring at Dave in that desperate way that a certain kind of woman in a bar had always stared at him.

Jared ordered a beer and after he paid for it Dave said goodbye to the women and the two of them walked over to the hostess and asked for a booth. She said there weren't any available and Dave sidled up to her with mock flirtation and said he was willing to do anything to get a good table. He was very tall and stocky and had a way of hovering over women that wasn't menacing but somehow endearing, or at least effective in helping him to get what he wanted. The hostess laughed at Dave while Jared rolled his eyes at her. Then she led them to a window booth on the far side of the restaurant. When she handed them their menus, Dave slipped her a ten, which she took, giggling some more. It wasn't Dave's money, Jared was certain, but his mother's. She always gave him cash when he came home and he'd spend it all in a night or two.

"How you doing, brother?" Dave asked him.

Jared sighed. "I'm fucked up. I'm having these nightmares about Ann that are awful. I would think maybe my unconscious would disguise what they're about, but they're so literal." The one that came to mind had appeared to him the week before: he was at his sister's gravesite and was trying to dig out her body, but the shovel he was using was small and plastic—a child's toy—and he couldn't drive it into the ground. In another dream, Jared was at Christmas Eve mass, sitting in the pew next to Ann, and she asked him why he hadn't wanted to sit with their mother, who was a few rows ahead of them. "She's been hard to be around," Jared said to her, "since you died."

"Your brain is probably overloaded," Dave said. "You know, your unconscious or whatever has too much material to do a bunch of rewrites."

The waitress dropped by to tell them about the specials and Dave chatted her up and then ordered some mozzarella sticks. She asked if they wanted two more beers and they both nodded and Dave said she could drop off a wine list too and she pointed at the table, where the wine list was sitting right in front of him, and he said, "Or we could look at this one," and she laughed. After she walked away Dave said he had to go to the bathroom and left Jared there, looking out at the other tables, mostly filled with couples he assumed were on dates. Denver seemed to be bursting at the seams with young people. In high school, Dave, Walter, and Jared would drive around downtown at night and there wouldn't be a car in sight. They would steal stop signs to put in their bedrooms, pay vagrants to buy them beer that they'd drink in one of the deserted parking lots on the west side of Speer Boulevard, or up at Red Rocks when the amphitheater wasn't in use. Occasionally, Dave would blow off Walter and Jared for a girl, but most of the time it was the three of them, trying to find something to do, even some way of getting into trouble, and failing over and over again.

The mozzarella sticks and new beers arrived at the table just as Dave got back from the bathroom. The two began to gobble them up. It feels good, Jared thought, to be able just to shovel food into my mouth. It wasn't really possible to act as much like a slob with the friends he had made in Boston; it was different with people you hadn't known during adolescence.

"Did you ever meet with that guy at Paramount?" Jared asked.

"He blew me off," Dave said.

"Sorry."

Dave had been working on the same script—a Western set in the future that he described as *Reservoir Dogs* meets *Blade Runner* and *Blazing Saddles*—about as long as Jared had been writing his dissertation, on pastoral motifs in the poetry of John Milton.

"Ah, it's just as well." Dave wiped a string of cheese off his chin. "I've still got the suspended license—you know, from my DUI?—so getting over to the studio would have been a pain in the ass." He chuckled to himself. "Hell, my mom dropped me off tonight. I felt like I was fourteen again."

The two of them drank their beers. Jared hadn't recalled hearing about Dave's DUI but that was often how his friend related bad news; he'd act as if they had already discussed something so that Jared wouldn't have the chance to ask him any questions and put him on the spot.

"We both had crushes on your mom, Walter and me," Jared said. "We'd try to drop by when she was leaving for her workout class, to see her in her leg warmers." He wanted his recollection to sound comical but his tone remained serious, in spite of his intentions, so the comment had a slightly creepy ring to it.

They were both quiet for a little bit.

"Brother," Dave said, breaking the silence, "I just bust up when I think about what you've gone through, what you're going through. You know I'd do anything for you."

"I'd do anything for you, Dave. Thanks for flying back for the funeral. And for calling to check in on me."

"Don't ever thank me for that stuff. Are you kidding?"

The waitress picked up the empty appetizer plate and asked if they knew what they wanted for their main courses. They both ordered New York strips with mashed potatoes. Dave asked her to pick out a nice bottle of wine for them, didn't even specify a price range, and she went off. He mentioned a party that a high school acquaintance, Mike Stans, was having and asked if Jared wanted to drop by.

"People will be cool," Dave said. "They care about you."

"I don't think I'm up for a party."

"Don't think about it. Let yourself go a little bit tonight."

Jared nodded. Dave was always telling him not to think so much, and in typical fashion he found himself thinking about whether or not he thought too much. "I was going to kill myself," he said suddenly, surprising even himself. "Last week, I found a first edition of John Donne's *Biathanatos* on sale for $1,500 at Devon Gray, this book store in Cambridge. *Biathanatos* is the first defense of suicide in the English language. Anyway, I considered stealing the book and using it as a suicide note, then sealing myself in a laundry bag and rolling into the Charles."

"Kind of a performance art thing?"

"Yeah." He didn't really think he would have done it, but at the same time, Jared found himself looking at his life frequently from the outside, in a way he never had before, and it made his existence seem flimsy and slight. Dave had attempted suicide in high school, hacking at one of his wrists with a pair of scissors—the real thing, or so it had seemed back then.

"That'd make a good scene in a movie," Dave said, "only the guy would have to decide once he was in the bag and underwater that he didn't want to die after all. Then he'd kick and struggle and finally break free and end up on shore, where a Juliette Binoche type would pull him onto the bank and nurse him back to health. The title would have to be something like *A Second Chance* or *Back to Life*. Then at the end of the flick he'd be diagnosed with cancer and die anyway, but see, then it'd be a tearjerker because the Juliette Binoche type would be bawling and the audience would have grown to like him."

"So I guess I need to find a Juliette Binoche type."

"We all need to find a Juliette Binoche type." Dave smiled.

Their steaks and potatoes came, along with a bottle of wine.

"They're going to plant a tree for Ann," Jared said as he chewed his food. The steak was delicious and for a moment he wondered if he should continue to eat it. Ann will never eat again, he reminded himself. She's rotting in the ground and you're eating steak. He set his fork down, then picked it up again. What was he supposed to do? How was he supposed to grieve? Should every act, every gesture on his part, be made in deference to Ann's death? Was that even possible?

"What do you mean?"

Jared looked blankly at his friend, having forgotten what he said.

"A tree?" Dave asked.

"Yeah, in the Botanic Gardens. A red jade. Isn't that weird. She'll have a tree dedicated to her." Jared wondered why he thought that was so weird, and decided that it was because it seemed like such a definitive gesture. In a literary work, a person could be buried and then the reader could learn that in fact bodies had been switched, like in Shakespeare's *Measure for Measure*, in which Jared vaguely recalled a swap occurring between Isabella's living brother and an already executed prisoner. But Jared couldn't imagine a tree being planted for someone and then everyone learning that the person in question wasn't actually dead. What would they do in that case, cut the tree down? And he wondered, as he had many times in the last few weeks, if asking himself this kind of question was perhaps a sign that he was losing his mind.

"That kind of thing makes our parents feel better," Dave said. "I don't know why, but it does. Let them have their tree."

"I don't have a problem with the tree itself," Jared explained. "It's just so sad." He was worried he might cry. "I don't want Ann to have anything dedicated to her. I don't want her to be dead."

Dave didn't say anything right away and Jared felt bad about almost losing his composure. He started to apologize but Dave waved him silent. "Don't be crazy, bro," he said, smiling at him.

As they fed themselves intently, the sparks of conversation became fewer and fewer. They didn't really have that much to talk about. They never had.

The first person Jared saw at Mike Stans's party was Walter, standing by the keg on the front porch by himself. "You assholes!" he cried when he saw him and Dave. "Thanks for the call."

"We just had some catch-up time, bro," Dave said. "Isn't it a little chilly to be outside?"

Walter grunted and poured them a couple of beers. Jared knew that Walter had been waiting on the porch in the hopes that Dave might show up, that he would rather stand alone and drink outside in December than enter a party by himself if the slightest chance existed that he might be able to arrive with Dave. Walter had followed Dave's lead since they first met on the playground of Dora Moore Elementary School. And in response to his friend's hero worship, Dave had always treated Walter like crap: making fun of him to his face, telling him to shut up, and in general ordering him around.

It wasn't much of a party. Mike was sitting on his couch with a girl Jared recognized but whose name he couldn't remember. When Mike saw him he just nodded. He must not have heard, Jared assumed. There were more people in the kitchen, some on the back porch smoking cigarettes and weed. A Grateful Dead song was playing in the background. It could have been a scene lifted straight out of high school only everyone, by Jared's account, looked a little thick in the face and gut. He glanced over the weird assortment of books on Mike's shelf: stuff by Nathaniel Hawthorne and Stephen Crane and Edith Wharton, all things assigned in high school, plus a bunch of Star Trek volumes and automotive magazines. When he looked up, Dave and Walter had drifted away. Jared went to look for them in the kitchen and ran into Hugh Emerson, a ski bum who had been in Ann's high school class.

"Jared! What's up?" Hugh slapped him on the shoulder energetically. The best Jared could do was ask about ski conditions—which Hugh reported as lame, except for Telluride—and then wait for the inevitable. When Hugh finally asked about Ann, Jared looked at him dumbly, then turned and walked downstairs into the basement without a word. Dave and Walter were watching four guys Jared didn't recognize play beer-pong. He told them he was leaving.

"We'll go too." Dave was already speaking for Walter again, just like old times.

"Don't bother. I'm just going home."

"No you're not." Dave shook his head.

"Hugh Emerson asked me how Ann was doing," Jared explained.

"That fucking idiot." Dave hit his palm with his fist. "We'll kick his ass."

"He didn't mean anything by it."

"We'll kick his ass anyway."

Walter nodded in agreement, flexing his neck, the muscles of which suddenly poked up sharply underneath his skin. "We'll kick his ass, dude, then trash his car." He spoke without making eye contact. Eight blocks he had to cover to make the funeral reception, Jared thought, and he didn't do it.

"Let's go over to the Cricket," Dave suggested, "look at the booty, then come back here and kick Hugh Emerson's ass."

"I don't want to go to the Cricket." That was the local hangout where everyone their age drank, especially during the holidays. It was the last place in the world Jared wanted to be.

"You're thinking, bro. Stop thinking. You have no choice. You are in need of booty."

"Booty," Walter mumbled.

"Please guys," Jared squinted his eyes, worried he might begin to cry, "please just let me go."

Jared began to walk up the steps and heard the two of them on his heels. He weaved quickly through the living room, relieved not to see Hugh, and out the front door. It had begun to snow. Walter and Dave followed him halfway to his car, at which point Jared turned around and held up his hands. "Guys, come on. I need to be alone."

Jared felt Dave's eyes on him, trying to gauge if his mind could be changed by sheer force of will, but it couldn't, Jared knew that, and when Dave realized it he acquiesced and gave him a hug goodbye. Walter tried to do the same, but when he stepped forward Jared suddenly realized he couldn't embrace him—that he was too angry—and just the fact that Walter had no idea made him angrier.

"Hey, you know something," he said to Walter, who was staring at him blankly, "Ann fucking loved you, and you didn't even show up at her funeral. You didn't even make the reception! What kind of bullshit is that?"

Walter stepped back. He wiped his nose with his palm and sniffled. His lower lip jutted out from his face. "Oh shit, Jared." He sniffled some more. "I don't know what to say. I just don't know what to say."

"Say you're an asshole." Dave pushed Walter in the back. "Say you're a stupid fuck."

Walter fell forward, his knees crunching into the fresh snow. "I really loved her, Jared," he said softly. "I loved Ann with all my heart."

Jared looked down at him as he gasped for breath. "I know you did, Walter. I'm sorry." He helped him to his feet. It didn't help to call people out on their behavior. Nothing helped. He thought of Satan's line in *Paradise Lost*—"Which way I fly is hell; myself am hell"—and got into the car. Before he pulled away, Dave walked over and tapped the window.

"Call me tomorrow," he said.

"I will." Jared smiled thinly. In some ways it felt like a night he would never forget, but in other ways it was nothing out of the ordinary.

Jared drove home cautiously, through the familiar streets of his childhood. He didn't have a car in Boston and figured he hadn't driven in the snow since high school. He checked his watch. It was barely eleven o'clock.

He pictured Walter kneeling in the snow, his shoulders shaking. His mother was right; some people didn't know how to handle death, but those were the people who were just distanced enough to be able to decide whether or not to participate in the awful rituals that accompanied dying: the church services, the parties. Other people closer to the epicenter of loss had no choice; they had to face it.

Having someone in your family die prematurely ushered you into the fellowship of the bereaved, Jared thought. People who had not similarly suffered stayed away from this fellowship as best they could because they didn't know what to say to a person grieving. But in fact, the horrible truth was that the people within this fellowship didn't know what to say to one another either; each mourner was consumed by his or her own grief, so the group of sufferers that wandered through the social world like emotional lepers wasn't a group at all; it was just made up of crippled people, none of whom could help anyone else.

After Ann died, Jared filled his apartment in Boston with plants: ficuses, ferns, hoyas, bromeliads, and other houseplants that he couldn't even identify. He bought the plants at Bread and Circus, the upscale grocery store two blocks from his apartment, and carried them back one at a time. He didn't know how to care for plants and systematically over-watered every one of them but that didn't stop him; he kept on buying them, stubbornly waiting for the little greenery they provided to make him feel better.

After Ann died, Jared also began to stockpile nonperishables: detergent, trash bags, canned foods. He had never cared for beans but he bought dozens of different kinds. He filled the once empty cupboards of his kitchen with boxes of coffee filters, family sized packs of paper towels, liters of olive oil. He didn't know what he was doing. He wasn't aware that he was afraid to go outside, where people died.

He became accident phobic. He worried about slipping in the shower, or electrocuting himself somehow—by mishandling the coffee maker, for example, or the toaster. At the same time he felt so cautious and paranoid, he also wanted to die, or at least he thought he did, so he came up with complicated suicide plans, like the one involving his laundry bag and a first edition of *Biathanatos*.

Stopped at a light, Jared watched a man carefully cross in front of him, balancing a pie tin in his arms. Living, breathing, keeping our hearts beating, our fingernails growing: we'll do anything to stay alive, Jared thought. We'll say goodbye to our favorite people and go on with our mundane routines because we want so fiercely to fill our lungs with air. In the face of death, we become greedy for life: selfish and hoarding. When he considered how tightly he had held on since Ann died he was filled with self-disgust and considered for a moment steering his father's car sharply to the right, into a storefront on Downing Street. But I'll never do that, he said to himself, and that's pathetic. To hold onto life like this . . . it isn't right. I should be dead. I want to be dead, but I'm too weak to do anything about it.

His eyes filled with tears. At the corner of Seventh Avenue, just a few blocks from home, he thought of the time—during a snowstorm—when Ann had taken him out in the old Buick and they had done donuts in the Safeway parking lot. It was unlike her to be so reckless, but it was like her too, to be silly and fun. I'll never be able to describe her to people who didn't know her, he realized. To them, she will never seem real. To them, she will always be my dead sister.

The next morning, when Jared came downstairs, Mrs. Reasoner was sitting at the kitchen counter, flipping through a home decorating magazine and drinking a cup of coffee. She asked about the night before and he said it went okay—that they had run into Walter and the three of them had hung out together like old times. Mrs. Reasoner had no response. He asked her where his father was and she motioned toward the garage.

"He's doing something with the recyclables," she said. "Is it the twenty-first?" Jared nodded. "The Shaunesseys' Christmas party is tonight. Sarah decided to invite everyone this time around, not just close friends. There'll be a hundred people there."

Jared pulled a carton of orange juice out of the refrigerator, checked the expiration date, and put it back. There didn't seem to be anything to drink or eat in the house; he wondered what they were doing for meals.

"I ended up at a party last night, Mom," he said, "and I don't want to go to another one."

"I don't either." She pushed her magazine aside. "I don't want to see a Christmas tree or open a present. I don't want to drink eggnog."

Jared sat down next to her and placed his hand gently on her shoulder.

She eyed him for a moment with the corners of her mouth clenched.

"What is it, Mom?"

"Nothing." She was silent for a moment, then gestured toward the window. "Of course, it snowed last night." Her mouth contorted briefly out of bitter sadness. "We don't deserve this."

Jared didn't know what to say.

"You know, your father's drunk. He drinks in the mornings now, out on the back porch. He keeps a flask out there."

Jared took in the information silently.

"I don't know how he's keeping his clients," she continued. "I really don't. Annabel"—Annabel was Mr. Reasoner's longtime secretary—"calls all the time to tell him of meetings he's missed, or to ask where he's placed important files. I worry they're going to fire him, Jared, I really do."

"They aren't going to fire him, Mom. He's been there for five hundred years."

"The old brokers are the ones they want to get rid of. They're the ones who don't know about biotech stocks, or how to check their e-mail."

"You don't know how to check e-mail."

"That's not the point." She squeezed her hands together. "I'm just worried. I won't be able to make it if we lose our house. I would die if that happened."

"You're not going to lose your house."

"We could. We've borrowed against it so much. All of the funeral expenses were so unexpected . . ."

"Come on, Mom." Jared had heard this kind of thing before, normally about his father losing money in bad investments, or not paying the bills on time, and yet the Reasoners' lifestyle never seemed to change.

"Just the other day he got called in by his manager and reprimanded. Apparently he screamed at one of the receptionists after he got back from a two-hour lunch. Even though he's been through hell, they can't allow him to make other people uncomfortable. That's what his manager told Annabel."

In the past, when the issue of his father's drinking came up, Jared always rallied to his mother's side, but that morning he felt pity for his father; he was the one who at least had to try to go to work during all this insanity. Besides, with the way things were going, why not drink? A part of Jared identified with, and even admired, his father's unfailing desire to avoid reality. But it was also sad to think of how much Ann had tried to get their father to confront his alcoholism—putting him in touch with counselors, sending him books—and how, with her gone, all attempts at self-restraint appeared to have been abandoned.

The back door opened as if on cue and Mr. Reasoner walked in, a little-boy grin plastered on his face: his tipsy smile.

"What's going on in here? Having a little breakfast?"

"There's nothing to eat," Jared said.

"Well, then, let's go out for breakfast. Let's go to a hotel downtown and get big omelets and pancakes. Grapefruit juice, doesn't that sound good? Maybe some home fries."

"I'm in my bathrobe, Glenn."

"You can change, honey; we'll wait for you. We'll go to the Brown Palace. I bet they've got a good breakfast."

Jared was silent.

"Just so long as we don't get one of those buffets," Mr. Reasoner added. "You know, I hate buffets: big feeding troughs—"

"I'M NOT HUNGRY, GLENN!" Mrs. Reasoner slammed her magazine on the counter and stormed out of the room.

"I guess she's not hungry." Mr. Reasoner winked at his son.

"She's worried you're going to lose your job," Jared said.

"She's always worried about something." He opened the refrigerator. "You're right, there isn't anything to eat."

Jared wondered whether or not to broach the subject and decided he owed it to his mother. "She's worried about your drinking too."

Mr. Reasoner walked out onto the back porch without saying anything.

Jared went home again three months later for spring break. Both his parents picked him up at the airport this time. Mrs. Reasoner had to drive because her husband had gotten a DUI the month before. He had not, however, lost his job, although Mrs. Reasoner was still convinced it was going to happen. "They'll give him a year from when Ann died," she had said to her son on the phone. "Then they'll let him go." On the way into town from the airport, Jared was tempted to point out to his father that he now had something in common with Dave, a suspended license, but he restrained himself.

The day after he got back, Jared and his parents had lunch and went over to the Botanic Gardens. The tree had been planted two weeks before in a small ceremony organized by one of Mrs. Reasoner's friends. The three of them had difficulty finding it. In the southwest corner of the gardens there were a number of benches and flowers and trees, all planted or built in memory of people. They wandered around until Mrs. Reasoner picked out the rectangular plaque that marked Ann's tree. She bent down, wiped away the thin film of snow that had settled on the raised letters, and waved the two of them over.

Behind the plaque slumped the red jade. It looked like a small bush, really; Jared wondered if his mother was right to call it a tree in the first place. He was tempted to ask his parents why it had been planted before the winter ended but didn't.

Mrs. Reasoner sensed his disappointment. "It'll get really big eventually," she said to him.

They looked down at the red jade. Jared had taught Milton's *Lycidas* the week before, for the first time since Ann had died, and he recalled his bungled attempt at explaining the Venus and Adonis myth. Students never got that story and now he understood why. Are we really supposed to believe, he asked himself, that after changing him into a flower so that he wouldn't die, Venus would still be happy loving Adonis? Isn't that pathetic compensation, to love a flower instead of a person?

"What are we doing for dinner tonight?" Mr. Reasoner asked suddenly.

"I bought a capon." Mrs. Reasoner stared at the tree. "We discussed it, remember? I'm serving it with rice and mushrooms."

"We eat so much chicken. I'm going to grow wings, on account of all the chicken we eat." Mr. Reasoner jostled Jared, who managed a weak smile.

Before leaving the garden to go home, they held hands and stood for several minutes in front of the red jade.

Whenever he went back to Denver, Jared thought of himself and his sister as little children. Ann's death was in these memories too but not in the foreground; it saturated the memories but it was itself not remembered. He thought of them holding hands as they crossed Sixth Avenue, or riding their bikes on the Fourth of

July, streamers tied to their seats, sparklers held in their hands. He thought of the small moments in the summers when they would have all the time in the world to themselves: time to finger-paint and play board games and snooze on the couch in the living room and pretend their parents' bed was a ship in rough seas and the basement laundry room was a dungeon. Time to feel joyous and irritable and bored. He remembered the two of them per-forming the complicated math required to calculate how old they would be in the year 2000, the year 2020, the year 2030. Their grandmother was already in her late seventies by then; surely they would both live just as long—get married, have children, grandchildren, their very own dogs. They did their cold, assured calculations in tandem, adding years to their lives as if they were jellybeans to be piled up indiscriminately and devoured at will. Outside, the elms' green leaves heaved in the breeze while other children played in the shade and pets slept on porches. All around them was life, lazy and languid: to be taken for granted and held loosely in their small hands.

The Iowa Short Fiction Award and John Simmons Short Fiction Award Winners

2005
The Thin Tear in the Fabric of Space, Douglas Trevor
This Day in History, Anthony Varallo

2004
What You've Been Missing, Janet Desaulniers
Here Beneath Low-Flying Planes, Merrill Feitell

2003
Bring Me Your Saddest Arizona, Ryan Harty
American Wives, Beth Helms

2002
Her Kind of Want, Jennifer S. Davis
The Kind of Things Saints Do, Laura Valeri

2001
Ticket to Minto: Stories of India and America, Sohrab Homi Fracis
Fire Road, Donald Anderson

2000
Articles of Faith, Elizabeth Oness
Troublemakers, John McNally

1999
House Fires, Nancy Reisman
Out of the Girls' Room and into the Night, Thisbe Nissen

1998
Friendly Fire, Kathryn Chetkovich
The River of Lost Voices: Stories from Guatemala, Mark Brazaitis

1997
Thank You for Being Concerned and Sensitive, Jim Henry
Within the Lighted City, Lisa Lenzo

1996
Hints of His Mortality, David Borofka
Western Electric, Don Zancanella

1995
Listening to Mozart, Charles Wyatt
May You Live in Interesting Times, Tereze Glück

1994
The Good Doctor, Susan Onthank Mates
Igloo among Palms, Rod Val Moore

1993
Happiness, Ann Harleman
Macauley's Thumb, Lex Williford
Where Love Leaves Us, Renée Manfredi

1992
My Body to You, Elizabeth Searle
Imaginary Men, Enid Shomer

1991
The Ant Generator,
Elizabeth Harris
Traps, Sondra Spatt Olsen

1990
A Hole in the Language,
Marly Swick

1989
Lent: The Slow Fast,
Starkey Flythe, Jr.
Line of Fall, Miles Wilson

1988
The Long White,
Sharon Dilworth
The Venus Tree,
Michael Pritchett

1987
Fruit of the Month,
Abby Frucht
Star Game, Lucia Nevai

1986
Eminent Domain,
Dan O'Brien
Resurrectionists,
Russell Working

1985
Dancing in the Movies,
Robert Boswell

1984
Old Wives' Tales,
Susan M. Dodd

1983
Heart Failure, Ivy Goodman

1982
Shiny Objects,
Dianne Benedict

1981
The Phototropic Woman,
Annabel Thomas

1980
Impossible Appetites, James Fetler

1979
Fly Away Home, Mary Hedin

1978
A Nest of Hooks, Lon Otto

1977
The Women in the Mirror,
Pat Carr

1976
The Black Velvet Girl,
C. E. Poverman

1975
*Harry Belten and the
Mendelssohn Violin Concerto,*
Barry Targan

1974
*After the First Death There Is No
Other,* Natalie L. M. Petesch

1973
The Itinerary of Beggars,
H. E. Francis

1972
The Burning and Other Stories,
Jack Cady

1971
*Old Morals, Small Continents,
Darker Times,*
Philip F. O'Connor

1970
The Beach Umbrella,
Cyrus Colter